If Only...

Helen Santos

Scripture Union
130 City Road, London EC1V 2NJ

By the same author:
Caleb's Lamb

© Helen Santos 1987
First printed 1987
Reprinted 1989

ISBN 0 86201 453 0

Phototypeset by Input Typesetting Ltd, London
Printed and bound in Great Britain by Cox & Wyman
Ltd, Reading

1

Dana Hughes was sitting in Dad's big armchair, legs tucked in, feet under a cushion. She was trying to keep her feet warm, but even the cushion didn't help. It's difficult to ignore cold feet, even though the rest of you mightn't be so cold, and Dana couldn't concentrate on the book she was trying to read.

Outside, rain was falling with such unchanging steadiness that Dana knew it wouldn't stop for a long time. The early darkness of the late December afternoon added to the gloom that even the bright living-room light and bantering telly couldn't dent. Perhaps it was because the rain, the greyness, and the cold feet so perfectly reflected how Dana was feeling inside that she was so aware of it all.

Supposing it rained for ever? Supposing it never stopped? Already it had been raining for several hours, no harder, no lighter, bleakly unpromising.

Someone had given David a big picture book for Christmas with the story of Noah's ark. Dana had already shared it with him several times so she knew it off by heart. The book was on the floor now, open at a page which showed nothing but a picture of flood water covering everything.

Had Noah looked out of one of the ark's windows, watching the rain, wondering what would happen if it never stopped? And had it been as dark and as cold and as gloomy as this horrible day was, with Christmas finished, both Mum and Dad out, and only the new term at school to look forward to?

Forgetting the book on her knees, Dana took some

kind of harsh satisfaction in watching the rain. She could have drawn the curtains but she wasn't in the mood to shut out the things that hurt her. She wanted to surrender to them. If life was always going to be so bleak she might as well get used to it. Even her cold feet. What did cold feet matter when everything inside was so much colder?

David was all right. Nothing made any difference to him. Whether he was having a good day or a bad day, somehow it was the same. His bad days spoiled everything for everybody but not for him. He could have his medicine and then he was all right. There wasn't any medicine for Dana.

This house would be like an ark if it went on raining and raining. As long as the windows were shut tight and as long as there weren't any cracks round the doors, the rain couldn't come in. There were chimneys, of course. But the fireplaces had been sealed up, so maybe the rain couldn't come in there either.

A house wouldn't float like Noah's ark. It was cemented to the ground. Once she went outside she would drown. But if she never went outside. . . . How curious it would be to live in a house under water. From inside it would be a bit like looking into a goldfish tank, only it would be all dark, with nothing so nice as painted shells and pretty fish.

The best thing would be never having to go back to school again, never having to be polite to the neighbours who made her curl up inside every time they asked, 'And how's your brother today?' Why couldn't they just forget that she had a brother? Why keep asking about him, anyway, as if her answer was ever going to be any different?

'They only mean to be kind,' Mrs. Hughes suggested when she exploded about it one day.

'I hate kind people,' Dana cried. 'I'd much rather they were mean and horrible and just left us alone.'

'I don't know which is worse,' Mum sympathised, 'people who just ignore you because they don't know what to say or . . .' Even Mum often ran out of words. 'They mean well, so try not to get upset about it,' she advised.

Dana wouldn't have minded so much if they really cared how David was but, funnily enough, whenever David was out with them Mrs. Lewis or Mrs. Hayward always just happened to be looking the other way, or they'd just decided to cross the road.

'They can't help it,' said Mum. 'It's no good trying to change them. They're just not used to people like David.'

People like David! Why did people like David even exist? And, if they had to, why did one of them have to be her brother?

Suddenly Dana knew that all her resentment against Mrs. Hayward and Mrs. Lewis really had nothing to do with them. It was all David's fault. If David didn't exist they wouldn't even be living in this house. If David didn't exist she wouldn't be dreading going back to school, seeing Fiona again. If David didn't exist. . . .

Dana squirmed in the armchair and the cushion promptly fell on the floor. She didn't notice because her eyes were blinded with sudden tears. Everything was David, David, David. He was worse than the rain. That would stop. She knew it would. Even Noah's rain stopped. But you couldn't stop David. He was going to be there always.

Mum loved David. She had a kind of passionate love for him that left Dana out in the cold. It wasn't that she didn't love Dana. She knew that Mum loved her, too. But it wasn't the same. Even in the middle of her loving Dana she was somehow thinking of David. Dana couldn't explain it with words. But she knew.

That was why this steady, gloomy rain was comforting. Dana sat there looking at it and it was as if the rain exactly understood.

Did Dad understand? He loved David, too, but not in the way Mum loved him. He was more on Dana's side, wishing that David wasn't there. He never said so. He never would. How could you ever say something like that? Perhaps it was even wicked to think it. But thoughts couldn't be stopped. They were there, and sometimes they got bigger and bigger in your head until you felt like exploding because you couldn't let them out.

The tears fell on Dana's book, a present from Fiona, all about show-jumping. She'd brought it on Boxing Day because it was Dana's birthday. She was now twelve years and three days old and she wished and wished and wished that the rain wouldn't stop falling so that she'd never have to go out again.

Her mood was broken into by the sound of car doors slamming, key in the lock, front door opening, Mum calling out, 'Dana, we're home!' and David echoing her, 'Dana. Home. Dana. Home.'

Dana jumped out of the chair, rubbing the tears from her eyes before Mum should see them.

'Nice and cosy, I see,' said Dad, coming into the living room behind the others, taking in the telly, the open box of Christmas chocolates on top of his newspaper on the little side table, and the book in her hand.

'You should have come with us,' said Mum, shaking the rain off her hair. 'We had a lovely time.'

'Lovely time,' agreed David, offering Dana the untidily rewrapped present he was clutching. His hair and face were shiny with rain. He liked rain and Mum had probably had to drag him indoors. His eyes were shining, too, and he shook the present at Dana, wanting her to take it.

'Thanks, David,' she said.

'It's a pair of socks,' Dad explained. 'Useful present. I always get socks.'

He grinned at Dana. She'd given him two pairs of socks for Christmas. Dad's grins couldn't be resisted, however much she was hurting inside. She smiled back and David promptly put his arms round her in a rough, tight hug. He was horribly wet.

Dad grabbed him. 'Let's take your wet things off, young man. Then you can watch telly for a while.'

'Telly,' agreed David, and allowed Dad to lead him back to the hall to have his anorak removed.

'Cup of tea, love?' asked Mum, pretending not to have noticed Dana's instinctive shrinking from David's exuberant hug. 'Everything went ever so well. David really enjoyed himself. I'm glad we found that place for him. I'm sure it's going to make all the difference in the world.'

They'd been to a Christmas party organised by the centre where David spent much of his time. It wasn't exactly a school. They didn't have ordinary lessons. It wasn't exactly a hospital, although there were nurses and doctors and people like that there. Mum really believed that David was going to get better there, but how better no one could tell her.

'Just better than he is,' Mum had tried to explain when she and Dad first told Dana that they were going to move so that David could go to this new centre.

Dana hadn't wanted to move. She liked her home, she liked her school, she liked her friends, she liked everything about her life which was just getting exciting because of Mrs. Gooding's Shetland pony.

'Can't David stay like he is?' she had asked.

She was used to him the way he was. She had never thought he could be different. How different, anyway? Even Mum wasn't sure.

When Mum had decided Dana was old enough to understand, she'd explained to her that no matter how much David grew he would never be more than like a child of about four. He could understand a lot of things;

he could say things, too, though he usually limited himself to copying what other people had just said. When he tried to say things of his own it didn't always come out right and then he'd get angry with himself.

He could walk, if that studious process of putting one leg forward, followed by the other, without being quite sure that his head and arms would obediently go in the same direction could be called walking. He even looked just like Dana, wavy dark hair, brown eyes, firm jaw and freckles. People often said he'd be a good-looking boy if only. . . .

If only his head didn't lollop; if only he'd keep his jaws together; if only his stare were not so frank, so uncomfortable to return.

He was two years old when Dana was born and by the time she was old enough to realise that her big brother wasn't the same as other children she'd grown so used to him being the way he was it hadn't bothered her much.

For a long time they'd been able to do all sorts of things together. Dana always did things better than David did and bit by bit, of course, she began to be able to do things David couldn't do, but David never minded. He was a good-natured boy, except for his 'bad days' (as Mum always called them). On his bad days he wanted to break everything, tear things up, and do the opposite of whatever he was asked to do. And he'd make a lot of noise and cry and not let Mum comfort him.

'Why does he do that?' Dana used to ask.

'I'm not sure, love. Perhaps because he can't let us know what he really wants. Perhaps because he wants to be like us and can't.'

Sometimes David's bad days would make Mum cry and once Dana overheard Dad say to her, 'Wouldn't it be better if we found a good boarding school for him? He could still come home in the holidays.'

'There'd be no one to love him there,' Mum had

replied.

'He's wearing you out,' said Dad.

'The trouble with David,' Mum tried to explain when she told Dana they were going to move, 'is that David won't stay like he is, He's growing up, the same as you are, and he needs to learn things we can't teach him, things that'll help him one day, when he's a man.'

Dana had never thought of David being a man one day. Although he was taller than she was, she was so used to thinking of him as her little brother that she'd quite forgotten that he grew older every year, just as she did.

Mum's words shocked her deeply. It didn't seem fair, David having to be a man. She couldn't imagine it, anyway. He was happy looking at picture books, playing games, watching telly, helping with very simple household tasks.

'I don't want him to be different,' she'd cried in protest.

'Don't you want him to get better?'

'Yes, but not different.' She couldn't explain what she meant but Dad understood.

'I know, Dana,' he agreed, 'but we've got to try to do what's best for David. And if it means moving to a new town and a new house, and you starting a new school and me a new job, it'll be worth it, won't it, if it'll help David?'

Dana had nodded, miserably agreeing, not daring to tell them about Mrs. Gooding's Shetland pony. But ever since that day she'd been different, too. She didn't have a little brother any more. Suddenly, she'd been made to see him with the world's eyes and the world said there wasn't a place for him as he was.

Somehow it seemed to Dana that there wasn't a place for her either and, whether he could help it or not, it was David's fault.

2

Dad called Mrs. Gooding 'the little old lady who lives up the road'. She lived in a large farmhouse surrounded by black barns and a couple of unkempt fields. She rented the fields to local farmers so sometimes there'd be a herd of bullocks grazing there, or a few sheep, which had to share with her own livestock – one black and white nanny-goat, poultry ranging from little guinea hens to a huge white goose called Fred, and the Shetland pony.

Dana's house backed on to one of Mrs. Gooding's fields, the largest one with an immense oak tree in the centre. Here the cattle and sheep would gather under its shade. Here the Shetland pony would often come, winter and summer, to strip the bark off the trunk when the field was covered with snow, but mainly to stand and snooze.

Dana's bedroom window overlooked the field and she'd watched him many a time, wondering what his name was, who he belonged to, why he was always there. He was a bright chestnut with blonde mane and tail that looked as though they hadn't seen a comb in years.

She would stand at the wall at the bottom of the garden with an apple or slices of bread and call to him. The sheep would come, and the cattle. The goat would have come but she was staked out on a long chain and could only bleat and let the others know that Dana was there. Even Fred and the chickens would come, but the Shetland pony always kept his distance.

He'd come part of the way, not to eat but just to inspect. He'd stare long and hard and see the bread and apples swallowed up by the others, but nothing Dana could offer ever persuaded him to draw near.

Dana had no pets of her own. David was allergic to cats, dogs, and all furry things, and it was no good promising to keep a rabbit in a hutch in the garden because David would know about it and want to play with it, too. Even standing at the bottom of the garden stroking the cows' heads could make his face swell up and go blotchy, so in the end Dad suggested that if Dana wanted to see Mrs. Gooding's pony she'd better stand at a different wall, where David couldn't see her.

One day Dana happened to be leaning over the wall trying to attract the Shetland when Mrs. Gooding came by. Dana had bought a packet of mints specially for the pony because a girl at school said ponies couldn't resist them.

'He won't take any notice of you,' Mrs. Gooding said. 'He's a wild one.'

'You mean a really wild pony, like in the New Forest or Exmoor?'

'No, he's not wild like that, but he's never had anyone break him in or ride him and he just doesn't like people. I bought him for my grandson when he was just a foal. Going for horse meat he was. Can you believe it, a little thing like that? There's no heart in some people. So I offered a pound on top of what the knackerman offered and he was mine.'

'What's his name?' Dana asked.

'Jack, or something. I can't remember now. You'd have to ask my grandson.'

'And doesn't your grandson ride him?'

Mrs. Gooding burst out laughing. 'My grandson's a six-footer. He's in the army. No, that pony's been running round that field ever since I brought him home, ten, twelve years ago.'

'Didn't he ever ride him?'

'He couldn't be bothered. He was more interested in

machinery than horses. Yet I got a lovely little saddle and bridle. Brand new. Still hanging up in the barn. You must come and see them.'

Dana had taken Mrs. Gooding at her word and she'd gone into one of the black barns which smelled of damp earth and musty hay and found the saddle and bridle hanging from a proper rack. Dust, spider webs and damp had attacked them but still you could see they were new.

'And won't Jack ever be ridden?' she'd asked.

'Do you want to try? I'd leave him alone if I were you. He's got a nasty temper. I used to try to bring him in of a winter, but I couldn't catch him. So out he stays and happy, too. Never had a vet to him yet.'

'If I could catch him, could I ride him?' Dana asked.

Mrs. Gooding laughed. 'If you can catch him you can do what you like with him. I like a plucky girl.'

'How will I catch him?'

'There's a head-rope in the barn. But. . . . well, never mind. You've got young legs on you and all the time in the world. Good luck to you.'

So Dana had virtually been given a pony to ride whenever she wanted. It wouldn't cost her anything. She wouldn't have to bring it home so it wouldn't upset David. Once she'd caught him and tamed him she'd be able to ride him every day.

She'd gone home burning with excitement, her head filled with plans. She was always reading pony books so she knew something about riding and caring for ponies. She'd very gently get Jack used to having her around. She'd very soon show him that she was his friend. She bought some saddle soap and polish and spent hours rubbing the years of neglect out of the smart little saddle which had never been used. And she practised slipping the headrope over an upturned broom so that when she tried to catch Jack she'd know how to do it properly.

The first time she tried to get into the field, the goose,

Fred, was so nasty to her that she gave up, especially as it was about to rain. The second time she went with a stick but Fred wasn't scared because he knew she had no intention of using it. The third time she brought some stale bread and threw it as far as she could, to keep Fred occupied. But he had eyes that could see backwards because hardly was she in the field than he was stretching out his neck, hissing and honking, trying to pin her against the gate. Her wellies could protect her legs from his beak but they couldn't overcome her natural fear of his outstretched wings and aggressive head. In the end she climbed back over the gate and went home.

'Aren't you riding that pony yet?' Mrs. Gooding laughed next time she saw her.

'Fred won't let me,' Dana confessed.

'Oh, that silly old gander. Don't take notice of him. Come up this afternoon and I'll chase him off for you.'

Fred was no match for Mrs. Gooding. It turned out that he didn't even belong to her. He'd appeared in the field one day and decided to make his home there. Mrs. Gooding decided she'd let him fatten himself up on her grain, then have him for dinner at Christmas. But somehow she forgot the first year and by the second it didn't seem a nice thing to do, though he was a nasty old bird that liked no one.

'But I can be just as nasty, see,' boasted Mrs. Gooding, as she went chasing after Fred with a broom handle, calling him all sorts of names. 'That's how you've got to treat him, my girl, or you'll never get across this field.'

Jack was at the far side, watching Fred's defeat with a certain amount of curiosity. He transferred his gaze to Dana when she started calling him. Then, when certain she was definitely coming to see him, he began to move away.

'Don't go,' called Dana brightly. 'I've brought you some mints, and an apple,' but Jack wasn't interested in mints. He probably didn't know what they were.

Dana followed him round the field for half an hour, never close enough to touch him, constantly aware of his flattened ears. His coat was thick and rough. She'd love to groom him and had already discovered that there were all the right tools in the barn. She talked to Jack until she couldn't think of anything else to say, hoping he'd get used to her voice, and then Mum began calling her from the bottom of the garden.

'Dana, it's getting dark. You must come home.'

'What were you doing in the field, anyway?' Mum wanted to know when she returned.

'Mrs. Gooding said I could.'

'Yes, but you want to be careful. Those bullocks might attack you.'

Although they lived right next to the field on the outskirts of a village, Mum wasn't really a country person. Neither was Dad, though he'd always wanted to be. When they got married Dad bought the village garage, planning to live in the country for ever, but Mum was too much of a city person and couldn't change her ways. Cows were attractive in a field, but not close to, and without her weekly shopping trip to town she often exclaimed she'd never survive.

She hadn't counted on the local people being so unwilling to accept them as they were. Most of the village social life centred round the church but Mum had no time for religion and said they'd only be hypocrites if they went to the services. Mum wouldn't even go to church for harvest festival or Christmas. She didn't mind giving things for jumble sales, or baking cakes, but she wasn't having the vicar preaching at her and didn't make him welcome on the few occasions he called.

Dad was all right. He spent most of his time at the garage and knew all the farmers and everyone else. Sooner or later they all called on him. Dana was all right, too. In the village school she had all the friends she wanted. Everybody knew about David though they didn't see much of him. Mum didn't like the way people stared at him when she took him to the village shop so she hardly ever went there. He didn't go to school but there was a place Mum took him to, miles away, where he had learned to walk and talk.

'The trouble about village life is everyone knows your business,' Mum would complain. 'You can't have any secrets.'

'I've got secrets,' Dana had exclaimed unthinkingly. 'If you don't tell you can keep secrets.'

Dad had laughed and agreed with her, adding, 'Mum's talking about other things. And what secrets have you got, anyway?'

Dana couldn't keep from blushing. Most of her secrets had to do with her friends, and didn't really count as secrets at home, but there was one thing she kept a secret from them both. She sometimes went to church, but she didn't tell because she knew Mum didn't like the vicar or anything to do with religion.

Dana liked the village church. It was about a thousand years old. The smooth grey stone, the dark oak pews, the big window with its brilliant reds and greens and blues picking out scenes from the Bible all combined to make it a special place, different from anywhere else. There were funny old things there – fading banners, plaques written in Latin, war memorials, brown photographs of previous vicars, and bits of stone that passing tourists would come to look at and get excited about.

In one corner of the church was a circle of little chairs where the Sunday School was held, and Vicky brought Dana to hear stories from the Bible and to draw pictures of Samson and Gideon and Moses in the bullrushes. Sometimes they used to giggle all through the lesson, especially the time the teacher told them that Abraham's wife, Sarah, had had a baby when she was ninety years old. They began thinking of all the old ladies in the village, imagining them suddenly coming out of their cottages pushing prams. . . . They were nearly stopped from going to Sunday School after that because they just couldn't stop laughing.

Sometimes Dana would go into church on her own, when no one was there. She liked just standing there. It was always so peaceful. It was a special place when there was no one there, and she didn't want to giggle then. She just wanted to be quiet and she always went home feeling warm inside. But that was a secret she wouldn't tell even Vicky.

Not telling about the Shetland pony was different. There was nothing wrong about it but she wanted to surprise Mum one day by riding Jack past the house and calling out from the garden gate so that Mum should see how she'd managed to tame him all on her own.

Mum's time and energy were so much taken up with David that she often didn't notice what Dana was doing. She always asked but when Dana started telling her something David would interrupt. Even when he wasn't interrupting, Dana could tell that Mum's mind was only half on her. But it had always been like that.

Dad listened, but he wasn't always around at the right time. However, even Mum would have to notice the Shetland pony.

Once Dana knew they were going to move, that Dad's garage had been sold and the new house bought, there wasn't any point in trying to tame Jack. She stopped going to the field, but she was angry and bitter inside. She didn't even say goodbye to Mrs. Gooding, scared that she'd burst into tears.

It seemed to Dana that nobody really cared anything about her as long as David was all right.

3

Dana sulked all the way through moving though not obviously enough for Mum to notice a great deal. Perhaps both Mum and Dad were so busy with the moving that they didn't have time to notice that Dana wasn't exactly enthusiastic. She couldn't bring herself to scream and shout and make a scene, which is what she felt like doing, but deep inside was the constant prod of her own thoughts, 'They don't care about you. They haven't asked what you want. They just suppose you're going to like it.'

When she dared to complain, 'Do we have to move? Can't we stay here?' Mum assured her in a very patient voice that living in a town would be much better for her.

'There's lots of interesting places to go to, clubs you can join, and so on.'

'There's clubs here,' Dana reminded her. She had been a Brownie and was now a Guide. There was a club run by the church, too, but Mum wouldn't let her join it.

'I'm not having them brainwash you with their old-fashioned ideas,' she had said.

'What about my friend, Vicky?'

Vicky was a good friend. They'd been going to school together since Infants and Dana dreaded the thought of starting somewhere else as a new girl without Vicky beside her to make her laugh. They'd already made all their plans for when they went to the Comprehensive, but Mum didn't seem to understand.

'You're bound to make new friends,' she said.

'No, I won't. They'll all have their friends from

Juniors and I won't.'

'It's going to be harder for David going to a new place,' Mum reminded her, as if that was the answer to Dana's fears. All she worried about was whether David would settle, whether he'd understand.

Dana asked Dad, 'Do you really want to leave here?'

'Oh, I don't mind,' he said cheerily. 'I don't like giving up the garage but . . . Well, it's all in a good cause, isn't it?'

But he didn't really look at her when he spoke and Dana knew, deep in her heart, that he felt like she did.

The new house was pleasant enough, though it was one of a long terrace and didn't look out over a field but over the back gardens of the houses in the next street. Dana had a bigger room than before, with some new furniture. She couldn't find anything wrong with it but she kept thinking of Jack and of all the plans she'd made.

She wrote a letter to Vicky but Vicky didn't write back and every day brought her nearer to going to the new school and she felt sick inside.

When they first moved in the neighbours on either side were curious. Mrs. Lewis came to ask if they wanted a cup of tea. Mrs. Hayward offered to fetch some shopping. They were very polite but they didn't quite know what to make of David who was very keen to make friends with them and certainly wanted to talk to them.

David's speech wasn't very clear. It was all right once you were used to him. You could guess what he wanted to say most of the time and you could be patient while he made his mouth the right shape for the words to come out. Dana didn't think about it but she could see that the neighbours were embarrassed and uncomfortable.

David was fascinated. He stared straight at them, just like staring at monkeys in a zoo, waiting to see what they'd say or do, and he kept saying, 'What's your name? My name's David,' only it didn't sound like that to them and they didn't know what to reply.

Mum was ever so bright and cheery as she explained why they'd come to live here, the centre for David, hope for treatment and so on. Dad tried to persuade David to leave the room but he didn't want to go and waved his arms about in protest, bringing startled looks to the neighbours' faces.

Mrs. Hayward remembered she'd left a chicken in the oven. Mrs. Lewis was expecting a phone call any minute. 'I only just popped in for a moment . . . If you want anything . . . just next door . . .'

'Nosey pair,' exploded Mum when they'd gone, relieving the tension she'd been under.

'They meant well,' put in Dad. 'We're used to David. We forget other people aren't.'

'Well, he's not a monster.'

'Of course he isn't, but you can't expect other people to see him the way we see him. People are frightened of things they don't understand.'

'You're always on other people's side,' Mum accused him. 'You ought to stick up for me.'

'I'm just pointing out that – '

'I know, I know. I'm sorry. It's just that they get my back up.'

'You're tired,' said Dad. 'All this moving. It's hard work. But we'll soon be settled in and everything will be all right. Won't it, Dana?' he insisted, giving her a wink of encouragement.

She loved Dad but she was feeling too churned up herself to respond. It seemed she was suddenly seeing everybody with new eyes, Mum as well as David; Dad, too.

Mum, always coping so well, even when David was at his worst, the day planned out like clockwork, nobody interfering in the way she ran things. Mum who was in charge and didn't care what anybody thought. She'd been on tenterhooks ever since the neighbours more or less invited themselves in – on the defensive, artificially bright. Was that just Mum today, because she was tired, or was that Mum and Dana hadn't seen it before?

And Dad, always trying hard to please Mum, even when he didn't agree with her – trying to protect her from David and from the whole world. Mum didn't seem the sort that needed protecting. She was the one in charge.

Dana was scared. She'd come out of the life she'd always known. The things that her life had been built on weren't there any more and somehow everything was different – not just the new house and the new town, but Mum and Dad, and David because he was growing up and couldn't be protected from the world any more.

Dana felt as though she had been flung out into the world, too, to a place where neighbours weren't necessarily as friendly as they seemed; where school might be an ordeal instead of a pleasure; where none of the children there would already know about David so that he wouldn't need to be explained.

This 'explaining David' was a new thing for Dana. David just was – part of the background of her life. Until now. Now David loomed larger and larger over everything she said and did. Her whole life was suddenly only to be considered in relationship to David's needs and his very existence.

It hadn't happened all at once. Dana's resentment had been slowly building up. Her realisation that David was something she didn't want and yet couldn't escape, battling against her natural affection for him, was hammered home bit by bit. Moving; losing her friend Vicky; Jack; seeing Mum and Dad as people and not just Mum and Dad . . . Hurt and bewilderment pressed in on her but remained a secret.

Fiona's visit on Boxing Day was the event that finally thrust the awful truth home, with a suddenness that left her without any defence.

Dana had never 'explained David' at her new school.

Outside school, none of the children knew her and the temptation never to talk about him, never even to admit to his existence, was too much for her.

Although she had lived in two worlds in the village, their boundaries overlapped. It wasn't just 'home' and 'school' there, but life itself that neatly flowed into separate compartments while being part of the main stream. In this large town, with everything and everyone new to her, it was far easier for Dana to escape her misery and confusion by stepping outside them once she went through the school gates.

Dana at school had nothing to do with Dana at home. Dana at school had stories to tell of Jack, the pony she had left behind; of Pony Club rallies and gymkhanas (all taken out of books); of coming to this new town because there wasn't a decent school in the village once you'd left Juniors.

Because she was on her own there everyone assumed she had no older brothers or sisters.

'You got any younger brothers or sisters?' she was once asked.

'No,' she truthfully replied. She could have stopped there but something prompted her to add, 'There's only me.'

'I wish I didn't have any,' said one girl. 'You don't know how lucky you are. You must have got a room all to yourself!'

Dana nodded and didn't even feel guilty. David was dismissed from her mind. Dana at school had no brother and it wasn't very hard to keep up the pretence. She never invited any of her school friends home.

Fiona replaced Vicky as her friend. Fiona was on her own in the first year, too. Most of the class had come up together from other schools and had their friends already made, but Fiona was a bit of an outcast at first, mainly because she talked 'posh' and had come from a private school. She and Dana were immediately attracted to each other and on the very first day Fiona confessed that her parents had divorced and her mother couldn't afford the school fees any more.

'But I don't care,' she said. 'It's much more fun to be at a big school, don't you think?'

Although Dana was pretty terrified, because she couldn't remember where all the classrooms were and hadn't been able to find the toilets, she enthusiastically agreed. There was safety in large numbers.

Fiona knew about ponies and gymkhanas so their common interest caused their friendship to blossom. Dana had read enough pony books to be able to keep up the pretence without difficulty. Thanks to Mrs. Gooding, she knew all about saddles and bridles and special polish, and she and Fiona drew pictures of ponies together and made plans to have one of their own.

Fiona was a girl who liked to be surrounded by others so she made other friends, too. She was generous with sweets. She knew how to make herself popular. She was pretty and dared to wear a hint of make-up although it was against the rules. The navy blue uniform looked nicer on her than it did on everyone else and she took a lot of trouble with her hands. Also, she was one of those people who always seemed to know what was going on – who had a crush on who; who was in trouble with the Headmaster and why. Even the teachers didn't seem to be able to keep secrets from Fiona and, whatever she found out, she studiously and cleverly shared.

Often Dana would find Fiona surrounded by a crowd in the playground, or the centre of a tight bunch in the classroom before lessons started. There'd be giggles and whisperings and certain people would be singled out for long stares.

Dana began to get worried. Even though she often enjoyed Fiona's gossip, she started to fear that one day Fiona would find out that all her pony stories weren't true. There was a hard streak in Fiona. She'd do anything for a laugh. Suppose she told everyone that Dana was a fake? It never occurred to her to think she could find out about David, perhaps because at school Dana herself so completely forgot him it was as if he didn't exist.

Even though there were things about Fiona that Dana didn't like, yet she was fascinated by her. She was so self-assured. She was a lot of fun, good at sports, good at lessons and willing to let others copy her homework. She was always good for a packet of crisps or a bar of chocolate.

Being Fiona's special friend gave you a certain importance and everyone recognised that Dana was that special friend. They'd say to her, 'Can you ask Fiona to do me a favour?' and Dana enjoyed having that kind of power. At school she was Somebody.

Then the Christmas holidays came. Fiona was going away to stay with her father and go hunting if she could hire the right pony.

'Do you promise not to forget me?' she demanded of Dana with mock fear. 'Promise you won't be jealous of me having lots of horsey things and people all around me.'

'I'll forgive you,' Dana agreed with wavering tone which made them both burst out laughing. 'But don't get carted.'

'Carted' was a good horsey expression for falling off which Dana had recently picked up from a new book.

Fiona pretended to be much hurt. They promised undying friendship in spite of not being able to see each other for two weeks.

'Two whole weeks!' exclaimed Fiona with theatrical dismay.

'You won't even come to my birthday party!' sobbed Dana. 'I shan't have one now,' which was how Fiona found out it was going to be her birthday on Boxing Day.

'I'll send you a lovely presie,' she said. 'My Dad will give me lots of money and I'll spend at least ten pence on you. Okay?'

'A friend indeed,' agreed Dana.

They exchanged addresses so that they could write to each other over Christmas. Fiona's address was somewhere in Somerset. 'There's a choice of hunts there,' she reminded Dana, who nodded knowingly.

But Fiona didn't write. Instead she turned up out of the blue on Boxing Day afternoon, grinning with excitement at the surprise she was springing on Dana, and with an airy tale about how Daddy had had to rush off to America on business and couldn't have her for Christmas after all.

'So Mummy put me in a taxi and sent me over here today because I was so bored. I could have been hunting. The Boxing Day Meet!'

All this as Dana, utterly bewildered, showed her into the front room where David was sprawled over the floor playing with his toys like any four year old, only he was already as tall as Dad.

Dana could only remember that afternoon as a nightmare. David was always thrilled when someone new came to the house and Fiona's brightness and laughter drew him like a moth to a lamp. He got angry when Mum tried to take him out of the room because he kept wanting to touch Fiona and kiss her, and his voice was rough as he shouted unintelligible words.

Just then Dana found herself hating David, hating Fiona, hating her parents, hating herself for feeling the way she did. She wanted to be swallowed up even as she stood in silent agony, seeing the astonishment and disgust struggling with an attempt to be polite all expressed on her best friend's face.

Once David got awkward it was hard to quieten him. He could be heard shouting in the bedroom while Mum and Dad tried to pacify him. Dana and Fiona stood looking at each other until Fiona remembered the present she had brought and handed it over.

It was a lovely book about horses, filled with colour photographs of the top show-jumpers. It gave them something to talk about. They had tea and Christmas cake and then Dad took Fiona home in his car.

Everybody apologised at least a hundred times and Dana wanted to curl up and die.

4

The day she had to go back to school Dana felt ill. Her stomach was churned up, her head ached. She had tossed restlessly all night with bad dreams, so Mum let her spend the day in bed, saying she'd call in the doctor if she didn't get better. The next day she was still in bed while David had his breakfast and was then taken off by Dad to the Centre on his way to work. Mr. Hughes was managing a petrol station now, which wasn't quite as good as running your own garage.

Dana heard the front door shut after all the goodbyes and David's resounding kisses, and then Mum went back to the kitchen for a while and came up to Dana's room with a cup of tea.

'You're going to be late for school if you don't get up,' she said.

'I can't go to school. I still hurt all over.'

'When will you be well enough to go?' Mum asked. She'd retaken her temperature that morning already and it was perfectly normal.

Dana's silence only confirmed what Mum already knew. Her next question was a confrontation.

'Why didn't you tell Fiona about David? It wouldn't have been such a shock to her then.'

'Why should I tell her? Why does David have to come into everything?'

'He can't help it.'

'And I can't help not wanting him to.'

Dana burst into tears and Mum let her cry for a while.

'If you want, you can stay at home one more day, but you'll have to go back tomorrow. Wouldn't it be best to

28

get it over with? Maybe it won't be so bad.'

'You don't know Fiona like I do.'

'She's your friend, isn't she?' Mum encouragingly reminded. Suddenly she put her arms round Dana and hugged her close. 'It doesn't really matter what people think,' she urged. 'Do you think I haven't had to put up with what people think? Even with Nan. . . .'

Nan was Mum's mother. She didn't have much to do with them. She'd always wanted David put in a home. Dana had once heard her say that people like David shouldn't be born and Mum had told her never to come near them again (she'd come to stay with them that summer). Nan had packed her suitcase and gone off the same day and they hadn't seen her since then. She wrote letters and sent Dana money from time to time, but she didn't come.

'It's easier for you,' cried Dana. 'You're grown up. And, anyway, you love David. It's different for you.'

'It's not easier, and it's not different, but is it going to help anybody if I go around moaning all the time? We've all got to do our best.'

'Why?' demanded Dana. 'Why can't we put David in a home? He'd get used to it after a while. Why do we have to put up with him?'

'You didn't use to talk like this!' exclaimed Mum, looking hurt.

Dana hated herself but she was hurting so much that she didn't care. Why shouldn't everybody be hurt if she had to be? Why should she have to keep on pretending?

'Dad's fed up too,' she shouted, horrified even as the words came flying out. 'You never notice. You only care about David.'

Mum seemed to tighten up and go all hard. She got up off the bed, her expression exactly the same as when an unwelcome visitor called that she was determined to get rid of quickly.

'You'd better hurry if you don't want to be late for

school. There's no point in staying at home. You're not ill and you're old enough now to know that things have to be faced, not run away from.'

She turned away. Dana heard her go into the bathroom and lock the door. She started crying again, so she couldn't hear if Mum was crying too.

School was as bad as Dana knew it would be. She was a bit late and had to make an excuse about not being able to get on the bus. Fiona didn't meet her eyes and for the first time Dana was glad that they didn't share a desk. Because of the way several in the class stared at her, she was sure the word had already got around.

When the bell went for break Fiona rushed out of the class with a crowd. Dana lingered and then found them in the cloakroom, giggling together. They all looked up as she came in and she knew they'd been talking about her. Fiona shot her a defiant glare and Dana turned round and went out.

The cold air of the playground helped her fight back her tears. She stood by the door taking deep breaths, numb with shame and rage. A minute later Fiona was beside her, determined to defend herself and quite unrepentant.

Her eyes gleamed challengingly as she began, 'It's your own fault. I can't stand people who tell lies. It's what you deserve.'

Dana could hardly believe this was her best friend. She'd seen Fiona in rows with other girls, cutting them with sharp words and clever remarks, sharing in her triumph when someone was crushed. Now it was her turn and she squirmed and burned and raged but, in her hurt, could only squeeze out a feeble defence.

'What lies?'

'After all,' went on Fiona as if she hadn't spoken, 'what difference does it make to me whether you've got a brother or not – and one like that! It's none of my business. But to pretend! Never to tell me. . . . ! And

I'm supposed to be your friend! You made a real fool out of me and I don't like that kind of thing.'

'Why should I tell you? If you were my friend it wouldn't make any difference about David.' Dana could hardly speak through her closed throat and struggled desperately not to cry.

'You didn't tell me,' insisted Fiona. 'That's the awful thing. You didn't trust me – '

'Trust you! You've told everyone about him. That's why I didn't tell you. And you've made people laugh. I saw them. You – '

'Jane and Chris asked me where I'd been over Christmas. I just told them the truth.'

'You're horrible. You're just angry because your father let you down, because he made all those promises and changed his mind.'

There was some satisfaction in seeing Fiona's face pale sharply.

'You make me sick,' she sneered in quick response. 'You're the one who's horrible. Pretending your brother doesn't exist. I wouldn't do a thing like that. I bet you wish he wasn't your brother at all. Well, you can't pretend any more. Everybody knows, and about time, too.'

With that she marched off and Dana was left on her own, shaking feverishly, feeling the icy wind hitting against her hot cheeks. She was too angry even to cry. The blood pounded in her head and she leaned against the wall as dizziness surged through her.

She wanted to go home. What would happen if she did, without getting a teacher's permission? But how could she talk to a teacher now? They'd want explanations.

Misery, anger, despair attacked her. There were crowds of girls all around, laughing, talking, fooling about, but no one noticed her.

Into her darkness someone brightly exclaimed, 'Are

you all right?'

It was Sandy Brent. Her real name was Alexandra but even the teachers called her Sandy. Dana always thought it must be awful to be Sandy. Next to being herself, being Sandy must be the worst thing that could happen to you. She was fat. She had spots, and even her teeth weren't straight. She had wires in her mouth. Just about everything that could be wrong with a person was wrong with Sandy, and Dana had been among those who made fun of her as well as sometimes thinking, 'Poor thing. How awful to be like that.'

And yet, people liked her. She didn't seem to mind the things she knew they said about her. She only laughed. She didn't have any particular friends but somehow Sandy seemed to be around when you needed help. Like now.

'Are you all right?' she said again.

'I want to go home,' said Dana, and tears slid down her cheeks. Once they started to fall she couldn't stop them.

'Shall I get a teacher?' asked Sandy.

'No.'

'Shall we go to the sick room? You can be on your own there if you want. And they might send you home if you're not well. I'll come with you.'

She linked Dana's arm in her own and Dana found a lot of comfort in being ushered along by Sandy who protected her from curious stares and half a dozen enquirers until they reached the sick room and shut the door behind them.

'What's happening here?' said the nurse who was having a mug of coffee.

'She's upset,' explained Sandy. 'She wants to go home.'

Dana answered all the questions, allowed her temperature to be taken, and at the end of it all felt quite foolish.

'Well, I can't see anything wrong with you but if you

want to sit on your own for a while, or with Sandy, you can. I've just got to take this mug back to the Staff Room.'

Then there was an embarrassed silence. Dana wondered if Sandy had heard about David. She longed to know if Fiona really had told everyone, or just a few of their friends. But she didn't want to ask. Had Sandy guessed why she was upset? She sat and looked at her in a strange way, which Dana couldn't make out. Why didn't she say something? Why didn't she say that she knew?

'I know why you're upset,' Sandy suddenly said, as if reading her thoughts. 'If you don't want to talk about it it's okay. But if you do. . . .'

Dana's face burned. She felt she could talk to Sandy and yet there was a hard anger inside her, a rage against Fiona, which caused the words to stick in her throat.

'Fiona's not as bad as you think,' Sandy went on after a silence, as if reading her thoughts again. 'She likes to pretend she doesn't care about anything. Everything's a laugh to her. She doesn't mean anything.'

'I hate her.' The words burst out, even as they had this morning with her mother. 'I bet she's told everybody. I bet everybody's laughing at me.'

'Everybody's always laughing at somebody when Fiona's around,' said Sandy, and Dana couldn't look at her, remembering that Sandy was often the butt of Fiona's jokes which she herself had laughed at.

'I bet you hate her too, really. Nobody really likes her. It's only because she's got lots of sweets and things. They're all creeps.'

Sandy didn't say anything.

After a silence Dana found the courage to ask, 'Was she really awful?'

'I feel sorry for Fiona – ' began Sandy, but Dana hotly interrupted her.

'Sorry!'

'I think she only likes to hurt other people because she's unhappy herself.'

'What's she got to be unhappy about?'

'Her parents, being divorced and all that.'

'It doesn't seem to bother her.'

'Only because she's always laughing,' insisted Sandy.

'She laughs at you, so how can you feel sorry for her? I'd hate her if I were you. I hate her now. She was supposed to be my friend.'

'It's wrong to hate people,' said Sandy, not in a pompous sort of way but as if she were really concerned. Even so, Dana was annoyed.

'Why, if they're horrible? Some people deserve it.'

'I know, but it's still wrong.'

'Why?'

'Jesus says we're to love our enemies and be good to those that hate us.'

Dana looked at Sandy in astonishment. Outside of Sunday School she'd never heard anyone talk about Jesus.

She was suddenly embarrassed. All her mother's hatred for vicars and do-gooders came over her in a rush.

'That's a load of rubbish,' was her blunt retort. 'You can't love people who hate you. Why should you, anyway?'

'Because that's what he did – love people that hated him.'

'Why?'

Dana's voice grew harder with every question. Sandy was red in the face now but, still braving the other's deliberate rudeness, she went on, 'Because Jesus loves everybody.'

Dana had no reply to that. She couldn't ask why again without sounding childish and, besides, she could see that Sandy was really serious.

'Do you really believe in him?' she asked instead, intending to make fun but not being able to resist some genuine curiosity.

'Yes,' said Sandy.

'And do you tell people?' persisted Dana. She'd forgotten Fiona, struck by Sandy's expression. She didn't know what to make of it, but she couldn't make fun any more even though she wanted to.

'Not always,' admitted Sandy. 'Sometimes I'm too scared.'

'Why have you told me, then?'

'I don't know. Maybe because you need him as much as I do.'

'Need him!'

Sandy's face grew even redder under Dana's demanding stare. Dana could tell it wasn't easy for her to speak. She was sharing something that was as deep as her own feelings about David.

'I hate being fat and having spots,' Sandy suddenly plunged on. 'You don't know how awful it is. My parents used to keep telling me it doesn't matter, but they don't understand. At least, I didn't think they did. Maybe they do. But it's awful. I wouldn't mind just being fat, or just having spots, or just a brace. But when it's everything! Sometimes I used to wish I could just die. I look at myself in the mirror and I'm a monster, just like Fiona says. Not even an ugly or frightening monster. That'd be something.'

She grinned, making Dana grin, too.

'Just stupid, fat and spotty. The typical fat school-girl that isn't only in comics. My Mum keeps calling it puppy-fat, but I'm too young for that. Really, it's something to do with my glands. That sounds disgusting, doesn't it? Vile.'

She was baring her heart to Dana now and Dana was feeling intensely ashamed, remembering how she had laughed at Fiona's slick remarks.

'One day I was standing in front of the mirror and telling myself, "You're vile, vile", and suddenly Jesus just said to me, "But I love you". And I knew he meant it because I could feel his love all over me and I knew he didn't see me all fat and spotty. He just saw me. Since then I haven't cared any more and it doesn't hurt when people make fun.'

At that point the nurse returned. Sandy's blush had disappeared and Dana's astonishment was expressed in her wide open eyes and trouble-free face.

'You're looking much better,' she exclaimed. 'Sandy must be a good nurse.'

She looked at her watch. 'You'd better hurry back to your classroom. If you're late tell the teacher where you've been and I'll vouch for you. Off you go, then. You'd better run.'

It was an order so they both ran, Dana in front. She ran as fast as she could, not because she wanted to get away from Sandy but because the strange mixture of feelings inside her urged her on. She'd never heard anything so weird in her life as Sandy's story and she didn't know what to make of it.

However, she forgot about Sandy as she ran. Rushing down the long corridor with an adult's permission was exhilarating in itself, as was having permission to be late for a class. She stopped at the door, waiting for Sandy to catch up and for the first time she didn't feel sorry for her.

Sandy was suddenly a person, not just a laughing-stock. She even had rather a nice face, once you ignored the spots. It was her eyes that made her face nice, the expression in them. They weren't hard eyes. They were eyes that cared.

They pushed into the classroom together, grinning, and were rather disappointed when the teacher didn't say a thing.

5

'Dad, I was talking to this girl at school today who says Jesus talks to her.'

'Oh, yes?' said Dad.

They were at the kitchen sink, sharing the washing up. Dana was washing, so she could talk without looking up. Sometimes it's easier not to look at someone when you're talking, especially when it's something important. She wouldn't have shared that information in front of Mum, knowing how she always blew up if anyone mentioned God or religion, but Mum was helping David with his homework.

At this new Centre they gave him homework to do, which had surprised Dana at first. Mum and Dad took it in turns to encourage him. Sometimes he really enjoyed it, like tonight. Other times he'd refuse to do anything and would start throwing things if you tried to force him. Tonight he was sitting quietly at the table, trying to match the plastic letters that Mum was taking out of the alphabet box, very pleased with himself every time he got a letter right.

'Do you think Jesus does talk to people?' Dana insisted in the face of Dad's non-committal remark.

'Not if he's not real, he doesn't.'

'He's real to this girl,' said Dana, remembering Sandy's earnest expression. She had believed her then, but now she was full of doubts.

'What did he say to her?' Dad sounded curious, but not mocking as Mum would have been.

'He said he loved her.'

'I suppose he would say that,' agreed Dad, 'if he

was real.'

'Why?'

'Because it's what the Bible says, isn't it?' He began to quote, 'God so loved the world . . .'

'But that's God and Mum says God isn't real. How do you know what the Bible says, anyway? Have you read it?'

'I used to go to Sunday School when I was a kid,' Mr. Hughes confessed as he dropped the dessert spoons in the cutlery drawer.

'You don't let me go,' Dana accused him.

'Well, it's a lot of nonsense, isn't it? We live in the age of science and technology. There's no room for God. He doesn't fit in.'

Dana didn't know how to make out what Dad meant. He sounded almost like Mum now – copying her – and yet she wasn't sure if he was being sarcastic about God, or science, or even just hiding behind Mum's arguments. He often did that. Dana knew there were lots of times when Dad didn't agree with Mum, but he always pretended to and just said what she said.

She was disappointed but she didn't know what else to say. Ever since her conversation with Sandy she wanted Jesus to fit in somewhere, but she didn't know where or how or even why. She remembered the village church, when she was there on her own and it was so quiet and peaceful, and she wanted to tell Dad about that, but she didn't.

He said, 'There's a football match on telly tonight. Are you going to watch it with me?'

They always sat together on the sofa to watch football. Mum thought it was dead boring and even David didn't like it, though he liked most programmes, so it was something that just she and Dad shared together which was really good. But tonight when she nodded she couldn't help being less enthusiastic than usual. She felt that even Dad was being swallowed up by David. He was so used to hiding his feelings, so used to not saying what was in his heart, that he didn't even realise that Dana wanted to talk.

'I'll do the pots,' he offered, knowing how she hated doing them, and the awkward moment was avoided as Dad took over and shooed Dana out of the kitchen.

Dana tried to concentrate on the match, but her mind kept wandering back to Sandy and Fiona and all that had happened that day. She forgot her disappointment with Dad as her heart grew angry again over her so-called 'best friend'.

It was easy for Sandy to talk about not hating people. She couldn't possibly know what it was like to have your best friend turn into your worst enemy. Fiona might have made fun of Sandy sometimes, but she'd never had a special relationship with Fiona, anyway.

Dana suddenly discovered that you could only really hate someone that you really loved, and she knew she'd loved Fiona. Being with Fiona made her forget all her problems. She'd invented a new world since she'd met Fiona, a world of ponies, holidays and fun, and plans to work with horses together as soon as they were old enough to leave school.

'My father will buy me a riding school, or we could breed ponies,' Fiona confidently asserted. She knew lots of people in the horse world who could get them into show-jumping or eventing, whatever they wanted. Now it was finished, and Dana was just left with David again. She could never make friends with anybody now. Everybody knew.

Mum hadn't asked how she'd got on at school. Mum was being very bright and cheerful, which meant she had forgiven Dana for what she'd said that morning although she hadn't forgotten it. Dana knew she ought to say sorry, but saying sorry was very hard especially when she didn't altogether think it was her fault. She was only saying what she felt. That was being honest, not rude.

She sighed deeply. Even though she could justify her thoughts they didn't make her happy. Oh, why was life so complicated? Surely nobody else had all the problems she had. And it was all David's fault.

These days she was finding it hard to be patient with him. It hadn't been difficult in the past. He'd been her little brother and she'd talked to him and told him stories and helped him build tower blocks that his jerky arms always knocked down. Then they'd laugh and start again. It was easy to make David happy. You didn't have to try very hard. You just had to want to and, except when he was in one of his unhappy moods, he was as eager as a puppy to play anything you wanted. The trouble was, he was as affectionate as a puppy, too, and kept wanting to put his arms round you and kiss you.

At one time Dana didn't mind. It was David's way of saying all the things he couldn't really say; of sharing his feelings. But now he was too old to share his feelings like that and had to be taught not to, and the affection that Dana had once enjoyed had become disagreeable because grown-ups found it embarrassing.

Dad suddenly shouted 'Goal!' in her ear, bouncing on the sofa and almost making her jump out of her skin. 'What a beauty! What – Hey, you didn't even see it!' he exclaimed, astonished. 'What's the matter?'

Dad probing was the last thing Dana wanted just then. How could she tell him? Surely he knew! And if he didn't, how would he ever understand?

'Oh, I don't know,' she suddenly groaned. 'I'm just fed up. Fed up. Fed up with everything.'

She jumped up from the sofa and escaped to her room. She vaguely heard Mum say, 'It's that Fiona business, I expect,' but her heart hammered too loudly with frustration and anger for her to hear Dad's reply. She tore off her clothes and dived into bed, pushing her head under the pillow. But she couldn't even cry because of the anger in her heart.

Some time later Dad brought her a mug of cocoa. He sat at the foot of the bed while she drank it.

'Try not to make things difficult for Mum,' he said. 'She's got enough on her plate.' He didn't sound angry, just apologetic.

'I'm not trying to make things difficult. I just wish – well, that things could be different.'

'I know what you mean, love. I sometimes wish that. And Mum. I expect David would like them to be different, too, if he knew how to say so. But we have to make the best of things as they are.'

'And what's the best?' cried Dana. 'It was better before. Why can't we go back? I hate it here.'

'You'll soon make a new friend,' encouraged Dad, sounding just like Mum. 'That Fiona can't be much of a friend, anyway, to make you so miserable.'

'It's easy to say that. She was my friend. Vicky was my friend. I haven't got any friends now and I never will have, ever again.'

'That sounds a bit dramatic, doesn't it? Never!'

'What's the point of having friends if I can't share things with them, can't bring them home?'

'You *can* bring them home,' argued Dad.

'No, I can't. Look what happened when Fiona came. It was horrible for her. If that had happened to me I expect I'd have hated my friend afterwards.'

'You should have warned her,' agreed Dad.

'Yes!' Dana's voice rose sarcastically. 'You'd better be careful if you come to my house because I've got this brother who – '

'Shush!' Dad interrupted sharply. 'He'll hear you. You'll upset him.'

'And we mustn't upset David, must we? It doesn't matter about me, as long as David's not upset.'

Dana couldn't stop herself. All the resentment was

flooding out again, sounding as ugly as she felt. But she didn't care. The tears in her eyes were as much from anger as from pain and Dad used the same voice to calm her as she heard him use with Mum when she started to get upset, so patient and reasonable that it just added fuel to her rage.

'You know how much he loves you. If he hears you crying . . . . And who knows how much he understands, anyway? Don't hurt him, Dana, just because you're angry. It's not fair.'

Dana didn't meet his eyes. Everything he said was true but it didn't help. It just made her feel worse. She swilled the cocoa dregs round and round the bottom of the mug, Dad silent because he didn't know what else to say, Dana still too defiant to agree with him though in her heart she wanted him to know how much she loved him.

Why was everything so horrible now? It hadn't been like this before?

Suddenly Dad said, 'Perhaps you can make friends with that girl you were talking about this evening, the one who was telling you about Jesus.'

'Sandy?' Dana was surprised. 'Mum wouldn't want me to be friends with her. She doesn't like people who talk about God.'

'Well, you can't take notice of all Mum's likes and dislikes. If Sandy's a nice girl then I can't see why she can't be your friend. Take it easy. Get to know her gradually. Does she know about David?'

'Everyone knows about David. The whole school!'

'That should make it easier for you, then,' went on Dad, ignoring her sarcasm. 'No more surprises. I think you're rather hard on Fiona. You didn't give her a chance.'

'You don't know her like I do,' disagreed Dana.

'But if you can't share things with her, then she's not much of a friend.'

'We shared lots of things.'

'But not David.'

'Why should I have to tell everyone about David?' Dana angrily demanded.

'Because he exists. You wouldn't keep him a secret if he was like everybody else, would you?' Dad was still being very patient, but Dana was unwilling to give way.

'I wouldn't have to,' she bitterly replied.

'You'll break Mum's heart if you go on like this. She does her best, you know. It's not easy for her. Perhaps sometimes she does get too wrapped up in David. But she can't help it. It doesn't mean she doesn't care about you and me. She does. She loves us both. But David needs her more than we do.'

'Does he?'

'You never used to talk like this!' he exclaimed. His patience was wearing thin, but still Dana wasn't willing to give in, to admit she was wrong.

She wasn't wrong. She wasn't. She didn't know how to explain it. She did understand what Dad meant, but she wanted him to understand, too. He didn't seem to care how much losing Fiona's friendship had hurt her. He seemed to think friendship didn't matter very much.

Didn't he know how much it hurt to have everyone laughing at you behind your back? Didn't he know about the looks that said more than words, the dread of walking into a classroom knowing people were talking about you? It was years since he'd been to school. He'd forgotten all those things. Or perhaps it had never happened to him.

'You just don't understand,' she cried out in anguish.

'All I'm trying to say is that you've got to learn to live with things as they are instead of trying to run away from them,' explained Dad.

'And if I don't want to?'

'Then you're going to find a lot of unhappiness.'

'You and Mum live with things as they are, don't

you?' demanded Dana.

'We try to.'

'And are you happy?'

'Not always.'

'Then why can't I try to find happiness my own way, with my own kind of friends, and not have to bring David into everything?' she demanded. 'How do you know it won't work?'

'It hasn't so far, has it?'

'And it hasn't your way either,' insisted Dana.

Mum would have been furiously angry by now and she would have left all Dana's angry questions in the air, without answers. But Dad was a calmer kind of person who tried to sort things out when someone was upset. His very silence now acknowledged that there was some reason in her question. Then he sighed and said slowly, 'Perhaps we're all wrong. Perhaps we all need to find a different way. But I wish I knew what it was.'

He gave her a hug to show he wasn't angry with her, but although Dana was grateful, there was still a kind of despairing defiance in her heart which made her feel hard, even against him.

It was a long time before she was able to get to sleep. A lot of things went through her mind, mostly things that added fuel to her resentment.

What was Mrs. Gooding's pony doing now? Was he still under the same old tree? Would anyone ever ride him? Was there any way she could get Fiona's friendship back, or was that finished for ever?

Last of all she remembered Sandy who said she had felt Jesus's love all over her so that she didn't care any more what people said. It had sounded so real when she said it. Could it be true?

She wished she could be like Sandy, not caring what anyone said, and being loved by Jesus like that. That must be something really special, if it was true.

44

6

Fiona had definitely cut Dana out of her life. Now Carol, who had always toadied round them both, was her friend. She and Fiona went arm in arm everywhere, sat next to each other at dinner and went off in the same direction after school. Everyone knew that Dana was 'out' and there were some who were really pleased about it.

Sandy befriended her and Dana stuck with her because she couldn't bear to be on her own. If only to spite Fiona she had to show that she didn't care, that she could manage perfectly well without her, so she deliberately sought Sandy's company and made sure that Fiona often saw them together.

Sandy was delighted and didn't seem to realise that Dana was putting up with her because there was no one else. Sometimes Dana wished she wouldn't be so eager to meet her at the school gates, or to save her a place at dinner if she got there late (which she tried to do occasionally, hoping to escape her). But after a while Dana found that Sandy wasn't such bad company.

At first she had been afraid that Sandy might want to talk about Jesus all the time. Even though something inside her was itching to find out more, something else was also dreading a further conversation. However, Sandy didn't go on about Jesus and Dana certainly wasn't going to ask.

It was quite a relief not to have to pretend with Sandy about anything, especially about David. Sandy wasn't interested in horses. She never watched show-jumping on television and had never been to a gymkhana in her life. So, although Dana couldn't possibly tell her that her pony talk had been mainly imaginary, in case Fiona found out, Sandy didn't respond with sufficient enthusiasm for her to exaggerate about Jack, even though she couldn't resist mentioning him.

Sandy had a little brown cat at home called Chocolate and that was all she knew about animals.

'A brown cat!' exclaimed Dana. 'I've never heard of a brown cat. He must be a tortoiseshell.'

'No, he isn't. He's brown. Chocolate brown. That's why he's called Chocolate.'

'Milk or plain?' asked Dana.

'Sort of in between. He's not light enough to be milk and not dark enough to be plain. He's just brown.'

This argument about whether a cat could really be brown led to Sandy inviting Dana home to see him and find out for herself. Fiona had never invited Dana home. Ever since coming away from the village Dana had been in no home but her own, so she went with some curiosity.

Mum and Dad were really pleased when they gave her permission to go.

'You see,' said Mum. 'I knew you'd soon make a new friend.'

Dana didn't point out that she'd said that before about Fiona.

Chocolate wasn't in when Sandy and Dana arrived. He had his own entrance, attached to the kitchen door, and came and went when he pleased.

'I did tell him you were coming,' Sandy assured her friend, 'and he said he'd be here. He must have forgotten the time.'

Sandy's mum said, 'Well, he'll be in soon. It's time for his tea. I expect when he hears the plates rattling he'll be in like a shot.'

Sandy's mum was as plump as her daughter. She looked a cosy sort of person, not so smart as Dana's mother and a good bit older. Her hair was grey. Behind her brown-rimmed glasses were the same caring eyes that Sandy had.

Dana was usually at a loss for words with adults. She so rarely talked to them. Mum and Dad didn't seem to have any friends and her only uncle, Dad's brother, was about as rare a visitor as Nan. But Sandy's mum was so ordinary and friendly that Dana very soon felt at ease. She was like an older version of Sandy, in character as well as looks (except for the spots and brace).

The kettle was already switched on, mugs were set out on the kitchen table where sandwiches and a home-made sponge were waiting to be eaten. It was only a little kitchen, the wallpaper faded and tatty, the chairs not matching, but there was a warmth and friendliness there which made Dana feel that she wasn't a stranger in this house at all and that Mrs. Brent already knew her well. When visitors came to Dana's house everyone felt uncomfortable and Mum was always on tenterhooks.

They went on talking about Chocolate – how they'd brought him from the Cat's Home a sick and straggly kitten and battled hard to save him; how even the people at the Home had told them to choose another kitten and not him; and how everyone, even the vet, said he was only brown because he was so sickly and weak and had no gloss to his coat.

'And they were all wrong,' laughed Mrs. Brent as she brought the teapot to the table and sat down with them and added, 'Let's just thank Jesus for our tea, shall we?'

Dana shut her eyes quickly, filled with confusion, thinking, 'Oh no. I shouldn't have come.' But then Mrs. Brent's calm voice began, 'Lord Jesus, we just thank you for being here in this kitchen with us this afternoon and for bringing Dana along to share our tea. Amen.'

She spoke so matter-of-factly, just as if she was talking to someone who was really in the room, that it almost seemed to Dana as if Jesus was there, only she couldn't see him because her eyes were shut.

Just then there was a bang and a 'miaow' and Chocolate had thrust himself through the cat flap and come stalking up to the table, tail stiff and high, wanting to know who this stranger was. He sniffed Dana's sock, just like a dog, but evaded her outstreched fingers. He was indeed a brown cat, with a pink nose, quite unlike any cat Dana had ever seen.

'You see, I told you he'd be here,' laughed Sandy as Chocolate sprang onto her lap and allowed her to give him a few bits of jammy sponge (because he only liked the jammy bits) and he stared at Dana with disdainful yellow eyes.

'I think he must have some Burmese blood in him,' said Mrs. Brent. 'They're brown cats, I believe.'

'But they're curly, too, and he isn't curly,' Sandy reminded her. 'I've a picture of a Burmese cat upstairs,' she told Dana. 'I'll show you after. He looks just like Chocolate except he's curly.'

The first thing Dana saw when she went up to Sandy's bedroom was the poster on the wall opposite the door showing a little flock of sheep going along a winding road, sheltered by tall trees and a grassy bank. There was a bit of mist on the road, though the sun was shining. Perhaps it was early morning. And there were words saying, 'Seek Me and you shall find Me'. The trees and the road reminded Dana of a road in the village. It was almost exactly the same, only she'd never seen any sheep on it.

'That's my favourite picture,' Sandy told her, seeing how struck she was by it. 'Do you like it, too?'

Dana just nodded. Sandy's room was covered with posters, all with words from the Bible. On the chest of drawers by her bed was a Bible whose paperback covers were curled up and whose pages looked well read. But it was the cat book that Sandy pulled from the shelf and which they looked at together, sitting on the floor by the wardrobe mirror where Jesus had once spoken and told Sandy he loved her.

In this room, in this house, Dana began to believe that Jesus really could speak. She couldn't have said why. She just felt it in her heart, but she couldn't bring herself to say anything to Sandy.

Chocolate came up and joined them. He started rubbing himself against Dana's arm, purring.

'He likes you,' Sandy assured her. 'Have you got a cat?'

'No, we can't have one. David's allergic to animals.'

'Gosh, that's a pity. I bet he'd like to have a cat or a dog or something. Did he like Jack, your pony?'

It had never occurred to Dana that David might be missing not having a pet and she'd never even thought of sharing Jack with him, though he might have been able to help her clean the reins and rub polish into the saddle.

Chocolate was on her lap now, pushing his head against her chest and digging his claws into her legs, but not too sharply.

'He doesn't do that with everyone,' exclaimed Sandy.

Dana was sorry when Dad came to collect her. It was a cold night, sleeting, but there was a warmth inside Dana that made her forget that Dad's car heater wasn't working properly.

'Had a good time?' said Dad.

She nodded, not wanting to talk about it, not knowing what to say, wanting to think it all out for herself. One thing she was sure of. She was really glad that Sandy was her friend.

Dana became a frequent visitor to Sandy's house. They did their homework together and Mrs. Brent would let them make cakes and toffee in the kitchen as long as they promised to leave everything clean and tidy afterwards. Sometimes Dana would stay to supper, when she got to know Sandy's father. He wasn't always there because he often went away to other parts of the country to talk to people about Jesus, and when he came back both Sandy and her mother would be full of questions about his time away.

Although Dana took no part in these conversations she didn't feel as though she was in the way. She was content just to listen. She'd got quite used to Sandy's mum giving thanks to Jesus for their tea. She still thought it was strange, but was no longer surprised, when Mrs. Brent might exclaim joyfully to Sandy, 'Well, the Lord's provided for that pair of shoes you need. We can go out and buy them tomorrow', or, 'You know that old lady your dad was praying with the other day? She's sent round a lovely cake for our tea. Isn't the Lord good?'

When Sandy's dad came home from one of his trips he would tell them what Jesus was doing in that place. He talked about Jesus as if he were a real person, dealing with people's problems, healing them, bringing joy to their lives. While Dana listened she forgot that Mr. Brent was talking about someone who had lived two thousand years ago, and he spoke so matter-of-factly that Dana knew these things really happened. He wasn't making them up.

Her heart burned within her when he talked about Jesus but she was too shy to say anything, too scared to draw attention to herself. So far, she felt comfortable in Sandy's house because no one – not even Sandy – tried to probe her thoughts and feelings. She was grateful for this because she didn't know what to think.

On the one hand there was Mum's antagonism towards anything to do with religion, and her father's unwillingness to give any opinion of his own. In the village Sunday School, although she'd enjoyed the Bible stories, she couldn't remember ever having really thought about Jesus except as someone who'd been good to everybody and did miracles.

She knew he'd been put to death on a cross, but she didn't know why. Mum said the Bible was a story book. Dad said he didn't know.

But in Sandy's house Jesus was always there. He was like a member of the family that Dana hadn't met, just as she hadn't met Mr. Brent for ages, until the first time she was invited to stay to supper. Sandy didn't keep talking about her dad, any more than she kept talking about Jesus, but just as Dana knew she had a father, so she knew that, somehow, she had Jesus, too.

'What do you do at Sandy's house?' Mum asked her one day, puzzled that she wanted to spend so much time there. 'Are you sure you're not making a nuisance of yourself? Why don't you invite her here for a change? I'm sure you ought to.'

Dana didn't want to invite Sandy home, not yet anyway. She still hadn't recovered from the hurt of Fiona's rejection and although she didn't believe that Sandy would react towards David as Fiona had, she still desperately wanted to build up a life of her own, without David. It was enough that Sandy knew about David. She didn't want her to meet him.

The good thing about going to Sandy's house was that she could forget her own. There was a kind of peace there that she could feel even though she couldn't explain it. In her heart she had a feeling that the peace in Sandy's house had something to do with Jesus being there, but she couldn't tell Mum that. She might not let her go there again.

One day Dana felt she just had to ask Sandy to tell her more about Jesus. Every time they went to the bedroom and Dana caught a glimpse of herself in the mirror she remembered what Sandy had said about Jesus talking to her. She longed for Jesus to talk to her, too, but he never did and she'd never asked Sandy what had really happened that day. The nurse had come back when she'd been going to ask and since then she'd kept putting it off.

She didn't know how to ask her, so aware that Mum would hate her to be involved in anything like this, but in the end the words just burst out.

'How does Jesus talk to people? You said he talked to you.'

The question didn't seem to surprise Sandy at all.

'He talks in lots of ways,' she replied confidently. 'There was that special day – the one I told you about when I hated myself so much – '

'Tell me about that,' Dana interrupted. 'Could you hear his voice? Could you see him? How did it happen?'

'It's not easy to say,' Sandy responded slowly. 'I didn't see him. And I didn't hear him, not the way I can hear you now. But as plain as anything I *did* hear him. He just kind of put the words in my head, but they weren't *my* words. They were his, and I just felt all warm and good inside, and excited.'

She smiled, as if recalling it all again.

'It was a bit like when my dad gives me a special hug, when he's been away for ages, or just before he goes. He doesn't always say anything, but I know he loves me in a bit more special way. Do you know what I mean?'

Sandy looked so serious and, at the same time, there was such a shine of certainty in her eyes, that Dana knew just what she meant. She nodded but before she could say anything Sandy rushed on.

'Jesus mostly speaks to me through the Bible. That's why I like reading it every day. There's bits that seem to be just for me.'

'How do you mean?' said Dana.

'Well, when he says things like "Don't be afraid". I'm scared of lots of things but whenever I feel scared I remember those words. It's as if he reminds me of them just when I need them.'

'And do you stop being scared?'

'Not always,' Sandy admitted, 'but I know Jesus is

52

there, looking after me and helping me. That day I talked to you in the playground I was dead scared.'

'Scared!' Dana exclaimed. 'Why?'

'Well, I always thought you were as bad as Fiona, being mean to people and so on. And I thought you'd say something nasty to me if I spoke to you. But you looked so unhappy. And then I remembered what Jesus said. "Don't be afraid". So I started talking to you. And when I told you about Jesus, in the sickroom, I was so scared.'

'Were you really?' Dana was amazed.

Sandy's face was red as she nodded.

'Was I really mean to people?' asked Dana.

'Sometimes.'

Dana knew it was true, but no one had ever told her before. She would have been furious if they had. But she couldn't be angry with Sandy because she knew Sandy wasn't trying to be nasty. She was just being honest.

'How else does Jesus talk to you?' she demanded, wanting to know everything now she'd started.

'Mostly I talk to him and when I talk to him I know he listens.'

'How do you know he listens?' insisted Dana. She didn't disbelieve Sandy. She desperately wanted to know for herself, only she didn't want to say so.

Sandy wasn't used to being questioned so deeply. Her face got redder still.

'Because he says so. He says if anyone is hungry or thirsty and they go to him, he'll give them food and drink. And he does.'

'How do you mean?'

'I don't mean real food and drink, though he gives us that too. I mean, when you're hungry inside for something. Are you ever hungry or thirsty inside? Wanting something badly, like when I didn't want to be so ugly?'

Dana looked down at the carpet as she nodded, not

wanting to meet Sandy's earnest gaze. There were things she wanted so badly. . . . David, Mum, Fiona. . . .

Sandy broke into her thoughts. 'When you talk to Jesus, somehow he puts things right. So I know he hears.'

Could Jesus really put right all the things that were wrong for her? The colours of the carpet began to blur into one vague pattern as tears forced themselves into Dana's eyes. She kept looking down, not wanting Sandy to see, but she couldn't say anything because of the lump in her throat.

'You can talk to Jesus if you want,' went on Sandy. 'All you have to do is believe in him.'

'It's easy for you,' Dana forced herself to reply. 'No one in my family believes.'

'They might one day, if you start. Jesus changes people. He's doing it all the time. He'll change you. He'll change them.'

'Can he change David?' There was anger in the question. What did Sandy know about having to live with someone like David?

'My Dad says it's a miracle when anyone is changed, not just someone like David,' said Sandy. 'But we can ask him about it if you want.'

Dana nodded. She wanted to believe with all her heart. If David was changed then everything would be all right. Perhaps Fiona would even be her friend again. She wanted that more than anything else in the world.

7

Although Dana wanted Mr. Brent to explain things to her, she couldn't help feeling scared and embarrassed as she and Sandy went downstairs to look for him. He was in the garden, taking advantage of the last bit of light before supper to plant out the baby lettuces which had come up in a pot on the kitchen windowsill.

'I hope I'm not putting these out too early,' he greeted them, 'but there's no more room for them to grow in this old pot.'

Sandy went straight to the point. 'Dana wants to ask you about David, if Jesus can change him.'

Mr. Brent obviously knew something about David because he didn't seem surprised by her words and he didn't ask who David was.

'How do you want him changed?' he asked as he went on pushing the soil round the lettuce roots with his fingers and making it easier for Dana by not looking at her.

Dana was so sure in her own mind that if David were different all her problems would be sorted out, but now the question was suddenly put to her she didn't know what to say. Mum was always talking about David being different but even she couldn't say what she meant.

In the end, after watching while Mr. Brent unhurriedly shook the last little lettuce out of the pot and prodded it into the soil, she said, 'I want him to be like everybody else.'

'You want him to run about and play football and do all the things other boys do, pull your hair, fight with you?' He suddenly smiled up at her, melting her awkwardness.

She nodded, already feeling more hopeful. That was exactly what she wanted. Then she never need feel scared of inviting anyone home again. Then Mum would have more time for her and everything would be all right.

'Do you know what one of our biggest problems is?' asked Mr. Brent as he straightened up. 'We always think that if Jesus changes everybody else things will be all right. First of all he has to change us. He has to change me.'

'But it's David who needs changing,' said Dana. 'Not me.'

'Let's talk about it in the kitchen. It's getting cold out here. You're staying for supper, aren't you? We'll talk about it then. I can smell something delicious that tells me supper is just about ready, and I must get my hands washed.'

There was stew with baked potatoes in their jackets. Chocolate had his own little plateful. He was the strangest cat who only ate what everyone else ate. Tinned food he completely ignored. At breakfast-time he had milk and cereal; at teatime some bread and jam or cake, and then for supper a little bit of whatever the family was eating was put aside for him.

'I didn't know cats liked potato!' exclaimed Dana, though by now she knew that Chocolate liked anything.

'No one ever told him he's a cat,' said Mrs. Brent. 'Perhaps that's the trouble.'

Sandy's father always said the prayer when he was at home and that night, after giving thanks for the food on the table, he especially asked Jesus to show Dana how much he loved her. They didn't talk about David. They talked about Jesus so that Dana could know who he really was – not just a man who had lived a long time ago, but God come down to earth in human form and who had died but come to life again to prove that anyone who believed in him would live for ever.

'My mum doesn't believe in God. She says it's just stories,' stated Dana.

'What about you?' asked Mr. Brent.

His gaze seemed to be able to see right into the confusion of her heart. He made her think of Sandy. When he talked about Jesus you could see he was talking about someone he knew and loved – just like Sandy – and his eyes showed that he wanted to share this person with Dana, too.

'I don't know,' was all she could answer, half of her longing to say she believed, the other half still resisting.

'Jesus came so we could know that God is real. He said, "If anyone has seen me he has seen the Father who sent me". That's God, our heavenly father. He made the world and he made us. And the Bible tells us that if we want to know what God is like we must look at Jesus.'

'But if he did all those miracles and things and everybody loved him, why did they kill him and in such a horrible way?' asked Dana. 'Why didn't God save him?'

'Because he wanted to save us. You see, Jesus came especially to die on that cross. He knew he was going to die, long before it happened. It was all planned, even before he came into the world.'

Mr. Brent paused to let his words sink in while he put some more butter on his potato. He'd forgotten about his supper till then.

He went on, 'All the wrong things we do, the lies we tell, the things we say about people behind their backs, the mean things we think about them, even the things we ought to do to help others and don't – all these things separate us from God. The Bible calls that separation "sin". It means we go our own way instead of God's way and that gets us into all kinds of trouble. It makes us do wrong things. It makes us not want to be near God because we feel guilty.'

Dana knew she sometimes felt guilty about things but she'd never stopped to wonder why. She thought the word 'sin' meant being wicked, like murdering some-body. She hadn't known that it really meant going your own way instead of God's.

Mr. Brent said, 'God sees sin as such a terrible thing that there's only one thing to do with it – destroy it! He can't pretend sin doesn't matter. He wouldn't be a just God if he did that. But because he knows we can't help being sinners, he sent Jesus to put things right for us.

'Where we ought to be punished, he's punished instead. He never did anything wrong. Even those who hated him couldn't find him guilty of anything. And because he was perfect – just as God is perfect – he could pay for all the wrong things we've done. But he had to pay with his blood. The Bible tells us that only blood can wash away sin.'

'It sounds horrible,' protested Dana, shuddering.

'Sin is horrible,' agreed Mr. Brent. 'When you look at Jesus on the cross then you can know how horrible it is. Ugly and shameful. No wonder we want to hide it away!'

Dana wasn't looking at Sandy's father now. She was afraid he might be able to see all the wrong things in her. Though his look was gentle she couldn't meet it. However, he still had more to say.

'The wonderful thing is that because Jesus died on the cross we don't have to pay for our sins. He's paid for them. He's put us right with God. We have to be willing to let him change us. We have to be willing to let him take over in our lives and go his way instead of our own. We can't have a relationship with Jesus except by coming to the cross and admitting that we've helped to nail him there.'

'And if we do want to, what happens then?' murmured Dana, still looking at her plate.

She was remembering a film she'd seen on television which had shown Jesus being whipped and mocked and then stumbling on the road because he was too weak to carry the cross they were going to nail him to once they reached the place of execution. No one had ever told her before that he had gone through all that for her sake!

'Then God forgives us,' said Mr. Brent, answering her question. 'Once we're forgiven Jesus comes to live in us and change our lives. We can't change ourselves. He does the changing, as long as we're willing to let him.'

'And can I talk to Jesus then? Will he talk to me?'

She saw Mr. Brent's smile.

'He wants you to talk to him. Every day. He wants you to read the Bible so you can find out more about him. He wants you to tell other people so they can be changed too.'

'What about David?' asked Dana, suddenly remembering why she'd started talking to Mr. Brent in the first place.

'It's funny,' he said. 'One of Jesus's best friends asked him that question. Peter. Have you heard of Peter, the one who three times said he didn't know Jesus because he was so scared, even though he loved him so?'

Yes, Dana had heard of Peter.

'Jesus was saying to Peter, "Follow me", but what Peter most wanted to know was what was going to happen to another disciple called John. "Lord, what about him?" he asked. And Jesus said, "What's that to you?" In other words, he was saying, I'll deal with John. Your business is to follow me. Do you understand?'

Dana shook her head.

'You let Jesus do what he wants with you, and let him do what he wants with David. You get yourself right.'

'Can't I pray for him?'

'Of course you can. We'll all pray for David, but you must let Jesus take over if you want to see any changes. You can't bargain with God. Don't ask him to change David before asking him to change you. Perhaps you need more changing than David does.'

Dana was astonished at these words but she was too

confused to ask any more. There was such a burning in her heart – disappointment because the things she thought were suddenly within her grasp (Fiona's regained friendship and no more the embarrassment of David) now seemed as far away as ever, coupled with the discovery that somehow she had played a part in the death of a man on a cross two thousand years ago. What she most wanted now was to be on her own to think things out.

Mr. Brent sensed her mood. He didn't say any more but got on with his supper which everyone else had finished. He had to go out afterwards but before he went he gave her a booklet and told her to read it when she was on her own.

Dana pushed the booklet into her anorak pocket, not really wanting to take it but not knowing how to refuse. She felt awkward with Sandy after that and pretended to be concentrating very hard on the homework they were doing together, to keep her from asking any questions.

For once she wasn't sorry when the front door bell rang, which meant Dad had come in the car to collect her. She was glad to get out of Sandy's house and go home, but she didn't know why she was fighting to keep tears at bay.

'Had a good time?' asked Dad, sensing how quiet she was.

She nodded fiercely.

'That's nice.' Then he went on, 'We don't see much of you lately. Sandy must be a very good friend. David's missing you.

He spoke in his usual calm way but Dana guessed that Mum must have been saying something. A wild surge of anger almost caused her to shake.

'David! David!' she cried. 'Why must he come into everything? Why can't he just leave me alone? It's not my fault.'

She was still crying when they reached home. Mum was very concerned and put her to bed and brought her a cup of hot cocoa. She kept asking what was wrong but Dana couldn't have told her even if she'd wanted to.

In the end the light was switched out and she was left on her own. She heard Dad downstairs say, 'She'll be all right tomorrow. I think something must have gone wrong at Sandy's.'

'She's at a funny age,' said Mum.

David was shouting, 'Where's Dana? Want to talk to Dana.' It sounded as though he was working himself up into one of his moods.

'Dana's not too well tonight, darling,' Mum began with eternal patience. She had a special voice for David which never sounded ruffled, no matter what. It wasn't as real as the voice she had for Dana and Dad. Dana was beginning to think that even David knew it wasn't real.

She pulled the quilt over her head to muffle his growing anger. She didn't want to hear. She didn't want to know. Here, in this room, in this bed – curled up as small as she could, knees almost touching her chin – David didn't exist. It was dark and warm under the quilt. She was safe from everything outside.

But although Dana could shut out David, she couldn't shut out her thoughts. They were inside her, part of her, and they wouldn't let her be still. She turned this way and that under the quilt, her thoughts becoming as muddled as the bedclothes.

Most of all she was thinking about Jesus, not because she really wanted to but because he wouldn't go away. It was almost as if he were there, waiting for her to make up her mind.

She wanted to say yes to him. There was such a deep longing in her heart to know Jesus the way Sandy knew him, but she wondered what Mum and Dad would say.

She thought she could tell Dad, but it wasn't telling

Dad that mattered. It was telling Mum. In Sandy's house it was easy to believe and know that Jesus loved you. Here it was different. It was almost as if there might be a sign on the front door saying, 'Not welcome here', which had made Dana clam up inside on the several occasions she'd been on the point of telling Mum about Sandy and how Jesus was so real to them all.

And what would others say? Perhaps she could keep it a secret? She would know. Sandy would know. Jesus would know. Why did other people have to know, too? It would be much easier if they didn't.

And what would Fiona think if she found out that she had become like Sandy? It might make it even harder for them ever to be friends again and she did so much want Fiona's friendship back.

From there Dana found herself remembering what Sandy had said about being scared to talk to her because she was as bad as Fiona, making fun of people. That hurt. No one had ever told Dana that she was mean. Was she really mean? Were some people really scared of her? Was making fun of people so bad, especially if you didn't really mean it?

Mr. Brent called it sin. Sin was a horrible word now that she knew what it really meant. Was telling lies sin? Mr. Brent said it was. She felt her cheeks flushing even in the dark as she thought of all the things she'd pretended with Fiona.

Fiona had called her a liar. But who was she to talk? Why was she home at Christmas instead of hunting with her Dad? Perhaps everything she said was lies, too. Perhaps she'd never had a pony, either. Was pretending lying? Was there a difference?

Dana tossed and kicked, unable to stay safe and cuddled up under the quilt as so many memories flooded into her head. All the little schemes she thought up to avoid being with David, to keep him a secret. Even the times with Vicky in the village when she'd lied about being in church and said she'd been doing something else and Mum had believed her. But they were only little things. White lies. They didn't matter. How could they?

If they didn't matter, why did they hurt her now?

Again the memory of the film she'd seen about Jesus came back to her. Could it really be true that all the mean things she'd said and done, and the lies she'd told, had somehow caused Jesus to be nailed to that cross to die? And if it was true, how could God ever forgive her for causing him so much pain?

Mr. Brent said that he did forgive, but how could he? She couldn't forgive Fiona, though what she'd done wasn't as bad as nailing someone to a cross. And Fiona hadn't forgiven her for not telling the truth about David. Really and truly, they could never be friends again, not unless Jesus did something to change things.

Suddenly, in the midst of her bewilderment, guilt and longing, she cried out, 'Jesus, you can change so many things. Please come and change them. Please. Make everything all right again, like it used to be. You've made everything all right for Sandy. Make everything all right for me. Please.'

Was that a proper prayer? She wasn't sure. Sandy's family talked to Jesus the same way as they talked to everybody else. But in church they used old-fashioned words which she racked her brain to remember and couldn't. She did remember one thing.

'Amen,' she said.

Then she was so very tired that she fell asleep.

8

The first thing Dana remembered when she woke up was that she had prayed to Jesus the night before. There was such a sense of excitement inside her that she made a special effort to be nice to David that breakfast time, pulling faces to make him laugh while Dad helped him with his cornflakes, and not minding too much the sticky kiss he was determined to give her before he went off in the car.

'You look happy today!' exclaimed Mum. 'It's nice to see you with a smiling face. Last night looked like the end of the world.'

'Never mind about last night,' said Dad, wanting to protect Dana from questions that might upset things. 'Let's just enjoy today.'

Dana was bursting to say, 'Jesus is going to change things. David is going to get better,' but she contented herself with just imagining them being a normal family, like everyone else. She couldn't really imagine it, of course. Normality had always been messy mealtimes, when they were grateful if David allowed somebody else to feed him so that it didn't take so long.

At lunchtime she asked Sandy, 'How long does it take Jesus to change things?'

'How do you mean?' was Sandy's puzzled reply.

'To make David better.'

Dana would have liked it to be instant but she didn't mind waiting a few weeks.

'Have you prayed about it, then?' asked Sandy.

'Last night. Before I went to sleep. I said my first prayer to Jesus and I just know it's all going to come true.'

'But . . . Have you got everything right between you and Jesus?' There was a tinge of doubt in Sandy's voice. She didn't sound as pleased and enthusiastic as Dana had expected

'Of course I have,' she replied impatiently. 'I wouldn't have prayed, would I, if I hadn't? What do I have to do now?'

'Why don't you start coming to church?' said Sandy, 'And reading the Bible? Have you got a Bible?'

Dana shook her head. 'My mum wouldn't want me to go to church.'

'Not if you really wanted to?'

'You don't know my mum.'

'You could come with me,' encouraged Sandy.

'I'll think about it,' said Dana, realising that going to church with Sandy couldn't be kept secret as it had been with Vicky.

The next time Dana went home to tea with Sandy Mrs. Brent gave her a Bible. It wasn't a new one. It was a paperback with tatty covers and curled up corners for which she apologised.

'It's only until you can save up and buy one for yourself,' she suggested. 'Or perhaps you'll get one for your next birthday.'

Dana started panicking inside. Where could she keep the Bible so that Mum didn't find it? She didn't like to say she didn't want it, but how could she take it home without Mum finding out?

'It's all right. I've already got one,' she blurted out. 'My dad's, from when he was a boy. I can read that.'

'Won't it be rather old-fashioned English? This is an up-to-date one that you'll be able to understand better,' explained Mrs. Brent.

'No, honestly. I'd much rather have my dad's. I like the old one. Really.'

Dana was certain that Mrs. Brent knew she wasn't

telling the truth, but she said no more and stopped Sandy from insisting that she took the one on the table. She felt utterly dreadful inside, wishing she'd never come, wishing she'd never told such a lie. The big paperback was lying right beside the fruit cake and Dana did her best to avoid looking at it. It began to seem as though even Sandy knew she was lying. She wished and wished she could take back the words, but now it was too late. Why had she ever said them? It was so stupid.

Perhaps Dad did have a Bible somewhere. She could look on the bookshelf. If he did, then it wouldn't be so bad. She could put things right. So she cheered herself up and was glad when Chocolate put in his usual teatime appearance and jumped up on her lap to demand a piece of fruitcake. There was no more talk about going to church, so Dana felt she could breathe again. However, she decided she'd better not go to Sandy's house for a little while, just in case.

There was no Bible among the books on the shelf. There was only David's book about Noah's ark which Mum had allowed him to keep because he loved it so much. He knew the names of all the animals in it and enjoyed pointing them out.

Dana had told him the story lots of times without ever thinking it was true, but when she went through it on her own for the first time she asked herself, 'Did this really happen?' She began to wish they did have a Bible in the house so she could find out what it said there. She couldn't ask Sandy without letting out the truth, so she had to stay without knowing.

Sandy brought her a present, a poster. When Dana unrolled it she saw it was the picture that had been on her bedroom wall, the one with the sheep going down the lane.

'I know you like it,' she said.

'Yes, but it's yours!'

There was such a shine of joy in Sandy's eyes that

Dana could hardly bring herself to look at her. She wished Sandy wouldn't be so generous and friendly all the time. She never gave Sandy anything and still hadn't even invited her home.

To Dana's surprise Fiona came and asked, 'What did Sandy give you then?'

It was the first time she'd spoken to her since their row but the leap of joy in Dana's heart was quickly overcome by a feeling of embarrassment. Fiona would laugh like anything at that poster and say something spiteful. So, instead of letting her see it, she rather offhandedly replied, 'It's just a poster. Nothing special.'

'Oh, all right then,' returned Fiona sharply, moving off in a huff, and Dana knew she'd made a mess of things again.

There was a moment when she knew she could still run after her, show her the poster, say she didn't mean it like that, but she held back. She just stood there, longing for Fiona to come back, such a mixture of frustration, anger and pain that if it hadn't been Sandy's poster she would have torn it to shreds there and then.

She pushed the poster under her wardrobe, where she kept her shoes, certain Mum wouldn't find it. She didn't have the courage to put it up on the wall and, just then, didn't even want to look at it, somehow managing to blame Sandy for her lost opportunity with Fiona.

The days went by and David was just the same. Jesus didn't seem to be changing him at all. If anything he was worse, constantly angry about things that he wanted to do and couldn't. He didn't want to play with Dana, even though she started to make a real effort, offering to do all his favourite things and read stories to him.

Mum said, 'I expect he's trying to show you how upset he is because you've ignored him so much lately.'

'Well, I'm not ignoring him now, am I? I'm trying to be nice. He doesn't want to be nice to me.'

It wasn't fair, putting the blame on her. Somehow,

these days, whatever she did was wrong. And her prayer hadn't been any good. Jesus just wasn't answering it. Perhaps he only loved people like Sandy who knew how to say and do all the right things. Perhaps he didn't listen to everybody. Perhaps he didn't want to change David at all.

Her hope was gone. More than anything else she wanted to ask Mr. Brent why Jesus hadn't answered her prayer, but she was scared to talk to him again in case he asked her about reading the Bible or going to church. She didn't stay to supper at Sandy's any more and made David an excuse for not going to tea either.

'He's being so difficult these days that Mum wants me home early, to help out,' she explained to Sandy.

She felt mean about telling Sandy lies, but it was Sandy's fault really for being so keen for her to go to church and all that sort of thing. She wished now she had never started asking questions about Jesus. Before that everything had been much easier.

It wasn't that Sandy went on at her. She was relieved that, in fact, Sandy didn't ask her any questions at all even though she was obviously disappointed when Dana stopped going to her house. But because Dana had this feeling that Sandy knew she wasn't being honest, she felt more and more uncomfortable with her and wished she'd just leave her alone.

One thing that did cheer her up was a letter from Vicky. In spite of their promises to write to each other they never had. Dana had let Vicky know her new address but Vicky hadn't replied. Now, all of a sudden, there was a letter asking if she'd like to come and spend a week of the Easter holidays with her.

For Dana it was light in the darkness. She began to remember all the fun she and Vicky used to have. They could go round all the old places together. Everything would be just like it used to. She could forget about Fiona and Sandy and pretend that nothing had changed.

Going by herself on the coach would be really exciting and Mum even agreed to buy her some new clothes for the holiday.

She started thinking again about Mrs. Gooding's pony and wondered if it would be worthwhile trying to make him tame this Easter. Perhaps she and Vicky could look after him together. It might be fun.

She couldn't resist saying to Fiona in an offhand manner that belied her real desire to share with her, 'I'm going to see my pony this Easter.'

Fiona just gave her a hard stare and made no reply.

Sandy's first reaction was one of dismay. 'Oh, you're not going to be away when we have our mission, are you?'

'What's that?'

'It's a special meeting at our church to tell people about Jesus. My dad is going to be one of the speakers and I really want you to be there to hear him. I'll be ever so disappointed if you can't come. When are you going?'

Dana told her and she breathed a sigh of relief. 'That's all right. It's three days beforehand. You will come, won't you? It's going to be really exciting.'

Dana didn't have the courage to say no. She didn't have any excuses handy and, besides, she was sure Sandy would be dreadfully hurt if she turned her down.

On the day of the mission, when Dana asked if she could stay late at Sandy's that evening, Mrs. Hughes hesitated.

'I was rather hoping you'd be here,' she said. 'Your dad's going out tonight with that chap from work he's been getting so friendly with. It means I'll have to manage David on my own, and you know how awkward he can be.'

'But I've already promised Sandy. It's a special occasion. She'll be ever so upset if I say no. And I haven't been there for ages, have I?'

Eventually Mum agreed, mainly because Dana wouldn't be seeing Sandy again till after the holidays. Dana wasn't sure if she was pleased or not.

Mr. Brent didn't have supper with the family that evening. He was already at the church and Sandy's mum said they'd have to get there early, too, because she was going to be one of the helpers with coffee and cakes. So it was rather a rushed supper, with a sense of excitement, and Mrs. Brent said a special prayer for everyone who would be in the church that night, asking Jesus to speak to each heart.

Dana found her own heart beating fast as she heard those words. She so much wanted Jesus to speak to her, as he had to Sandy, but so far he hadn't. Would he answer her prayer tonight? Would she go home and find David changed?

Sandy's church was very different to the one in the village. It didn't have any stained glass windows or old stone walls with plaques and banners. It didn't have an altar with cross and candlesticks. It was just like a school hall, with a raised platform at one end and a gallery at the other, and there weren't even any pews. Instead there were rows and rows of blue chairs. The choir on the platform weren't dressed in long robes, as in the village. They were wearing their ordinary clothes and, as the seats began to fill up, they started singing lively songs about Jesus while someone played the guitar.

Sandy and Dana were in the gallery. 'We can see everything better from up here,' Sandy promised, though Dana didn't know what they were going to see.

It was quite good fun watching people come in and fill up the seats, and change their minds and go and sit somewhere else. Song sheets were being given out and people started to join in the singing. A few small children ran about and several old ladies with hats, macs, wet umbrellas and bags took a lot of settling in their places.

Mum always said that nobody went to church these

days so Dana was surprised to see so many people coming in. She and Sandy got busy trying to count everybody, leaning over the balcony rail, and Dana was suddenly taken aback as Dad walked into sight with another man and sat down on the left side of the hall. His back was towards her so he couldn't see her unless he turned round and started staring about, so Dana sat down hurriedly, filled with confusion.

'What's the matter?' exclaimed Sandy, seeing her so red and silent, but at that moment someone on the platform started speaking into the microphone and she had to be quiet.

There were prayers and more songs and other people talking before Mr. Brent, who'd been sitting quietly on the platform, got up to speak, but Dana hardly took anything in, wondering how it was that Dad could be sitting downstairs. Did Mum know he was at the mission? Was he going to tell her if she didn't? She didn't tell Sandy he was there. She didn't want her to know and she sank as far back in her seat as she could, hoping Dad wouldn't see her. Why were things always going wrong?

Mr. Brent's voice that she knew so well sounded exactly as it always did. It didn't seem as though he was talking to a whole crowd of people. It seemed as though he was talking to her across the kitchen table and everyone else just happened to be there.

To Dana's amazement he said he was going to talk about Noah's ark. Everyone laughed when he referred to the rain that had been soaking people in unexpected showers all day and which had been steadily falling for the last hour, but Dana didn't laugh. Her heart was beating too fast.

She couldn't understand everything Mr. Brent said though he spoke simply and quietly. He spoke about a God whose heart was filled with pain because men were so wicked and full of violence. And the only solution was to destroy them all because not one of them was good.

And he spoke about one man who was good – Noah, who was righteous and blameless, who did nothing wrong. He described how everyone must have laughed at Noah when he started building his gigantic boat, a long way from the sea.

'Not a little boat, like the ones in story books, but as big as a transatlantic liner.'

He spoke about a God who was too mysterious and mighty to be understood, who could talk to all the wild animals and persuade them to come to Noah and trust him and go into that great ship. And he talked about Noah's sons and their wives and children, who weren't good at all but who were willing to believe what Noah said, in spite of how ridiculous it seemed, and to enter the ark with him before there was even a cloud in the sky and no water for the ship to float on.

'That's faith,' he said.

Then he started talking about Jesus, comparing him to Noah, able to save those who deserved to be destroyed because they trusted in him. He said Jesus was like that big ship, too. Everyone in that ship was safe. God had shut them in and nothing bad could happen to them.

'I wonder how many people here tonight know that they are safe?' he asked, his searching gaze seeming to take in everyone there, including Dana. 'If that rain outside didn't stop, if we were all drowned tonight, how many of us would be safe? How many of us are willing to be laughed at as we take a step of faith?'

Then people were told to go forward if they wanted to get right with God through Jesus. For a long while it looked as though nobody wanted to until a boy a couple of years older than Dana stood up and walked to the front. While someone came to speak to him two ladies and a man got up, too.

Dana's heart seemed as though it was going to burst.

She wanted to go down but she was so far away in the gallery and how would she ever have the courage to walk all that way on her own? She half stood up. Perhaps Sandy would come with her, but then she saw a movement downstairs as another man suddenly rose and joined the others at the front. It was Dad.

'Do you want to go down?' she heard Sandy say.

Frozen with surprise, she shook her head and sat back in her seat. She couldn't take her eyes off Dad. Mr. Brent was talking to him and suddenly she realised from the way Dad's shoulders were shaking that he was crying.

It was terrible. Men didn't cry. Mum cried sometimes, but not Dad. Dad couldn't cry. What did Jesus do to people to make them act like that?

9

Staying with Vicky was like escaping back into a time before life had become so complicated and confused. Vicky was an only child, so sharing with Dana was a novelty, and Dana enjoyed being the centre of attention as Vicky's parents did all they could to make her feel welcome.

They had lots to talk about; the new schools, the people who'd bought the garage, the couple living in the cottage. Dana told Vicky about Fiona, about her ponies and their plan for having a riding school of their own one day. She didn't tell her they were no longer friends and she didn't mention Sandy at all.

Vicky had made all sorts of plans for picnics and midnight feasts, the latter being a secret, of course, and at first it was easy for Dana to slip back into feeling as though the last nine months or so were hardly more than a bad dream.

It was no good keeping Mrs. Gooding's pony a secret now and they went together to see him. It was strange walking past Dana's old home, knowing that someone else lived there. It looked the same. The curtains hadn't been changed and the same daffodils were scattered in bunches round the garden.

They looked over the field wall and were relieved to see that Jack was still there, looking just the same, his coat rough and long. his tail thick and untidy, grazing aloof from the few bullocks and the dozen or so ewes, each of which had a lamb or two. For a while they leaned over the wall, calling both to Jack and the lambs. Jack didn't even twitch an ear or look in their direction. The lambs stood and stared, intensely curious, but none was bold enough to come close.

Vicky confessed to being half scared of Mrs. Gooding. 'I always thought she was a witch,' she said, 'going round on a broomstick at night, casting spells and things.'

Dana liked the way Vicky made up stories about people and imagined them doing all sorts of weird things. No one was ordinary in Vicky's mind, so it was hardly surprising that Mrs. Gooding should be a witch as soon as the sun went down.

They went giggling up to the gate, pretending to be scared, not even sure if they ought to be on Mrs. Gooding's property without permission.

'I bet Fred is really a person, an old man who crossed her one day,' whispered Vicky. 'That's really why she doesn't eat him, not because she cares about him but because she'd be a cannibal if she did.'

'What about Jack then? Do you think he's really a pony or do you think something happened to him?'

'Something happened to him,' stated Vicky confidently. 'There used to be a little boy called Jack whose father made tombstones for the church. And Jack one day saw Mrs. Gooding casting spells in the moonlight. He was supposed to be in bed but he'd heard strange sounds in the churchyard and come out to investigate. He was never seen again, and that's when Mrs. Gooding came back from market with a chestnut foal. . . .' Her voice wandered off into a dramatic silence.

'What would she change us into if she caught us trespassing?' Dana wondered.

'Hens!' said Vicky with great certainty, pointing to the little flock that was pecking and clucking its way round the edge of the field. They spent the next ten minutes trying to decide which hen was who, and then who the nanny goat could possibly be.

James, the guard dog, started to bark and Mrs. Gooding came to the door. She remembered Dana and her promise. 'But a week's not long enough to do anything,' she said. 'Old Jack won't change his ways now. He's like me. Got a mind of his own.'

In spite of her words both Dana and Vicky tried to persuade Jack to be caught. When they got too close he kicked his little back hoofs at them and when he was tired of circling the field he stood his ground and defied them with flattened ears and bared teeth.

'You'd think if he was the gravedigger's son he'd want to be rescued,' said Dana, not without some annoyance. She'd forgotten what a horrible pony Jack really was and had almost come to believe the stories she'd told Fiona about him.

'He's forgotten,' said Vicky. 'It's all part of the spell.'

Vicky quickly lost interest in Jack and Dana might not have bothered about him again except that one morning Vicky had to go to the dentist and Dana said she'd pay one more visit to Jack while she was there. They made all sorts of plans of how Vicky would recognise her if she was turned into a hen, and then went on to the more interesting plans of what food supplies Vicky could bring back from the supermarket for their midnight feast.

It turned out to be a wet morning but Dana still decided to go and see Jack. She'd brought her anorak and wellingtons so a bit of rain didn't matter. Going up the lane on her own was different from going with Vicky. It was like going home, and there was a sudden pain in her heart as she stopped outside the front gate, thinking back.

Why was everything so different now, when it hadn't been before? Mum had said things would be better when they moved, but they weren't. They were worse.

The confusion and heaviness that she'd managed to push aside in Vicky's company suddenly came back. Dad hadn't said a word about the mission, even though Dana had expected him to. He still didn't know she had been there and because both of them were keeping a secret Dana had hardly known how to talk to him.

And what had happened at that meeting, anyway, that had made Dad cry? That was the worst thing, seeing him cry. She'd tried so hard to shut the memory out of her mind and had longed for Dad to say something about what had happened so that she could understand.

Was he as scared of Mum's reaction as she was? Would he be too scared to get a Bible or go to church? Was wanting to know Jesus always as complicated and hard as this? And was it worth it? Did he really answer prayer, anybody's prayer, or was it only special people like Sandy and her family?

Whenever Dana was on her own these thoughts kept coming back to her, even though she didn't want them to. It was as if she couldn't stop thinking about Jesus, as if he were determined to get into her life – her family's life – one way or another.

If only Mum wouldn't mind. . . . If only she didn't get so angry when anyone talked about God. . . . Dad didn't like to upset her, so perhaps he'd never say anything. And if he didn't, how could Dana ever tell him what she'd seen or ask him what had happened?

The bleating of lambs broke into her thoughts. She'd only stopped at the gate for a moment but time stands still when you're thinking.

Although James barked and Fred made a beeline to attack her, honking loudly, Mrs. Gooding didn't appear. Having to deal with Fred on her own, heart beating fast, Dana was able to escape her thoughts more easily than Fred's hisses and beating wings. She tossed him a peppermint and, while he stopped to examine it, was able to put enough distance between herself and him to feel safe.

Jack obviously cared nothing about the rain. Instead of sheltering under the oak tree he was at the far side of the field. He laid back his ears the moment he saw Dana, tossing his head in a menacing fashion.

Anger surged in Dana's heart against him. He wasn't a bit like any of the ponies in books who, sooner or later, did everything their owners wanted. He was a real pony, not a story book one and nothing would ever change him. She was wet and muddy. A cold wind was blowing, too, and it was utterly stupid to be in this field, in the pouring rain, offering friendship to a pony that neither wanted nor needed it. The time she had wasted in both dreams and effort!

At that moment the rain began to fall even more heavily. She decided to shelter in the barn before getting back to Vicky's house. It might stop after a while. But she still had to face Fred again! What an idiot she was.

The barn door was open. Mrs. Gooding was there.

'I thought it might be you,' she greeted Dana. 'I heard Fred. She's after that pony again, I told myself. Well, she'll learn, I said.'

Dana felt like saying something sarcastic but, as well as not knowing quite what to say, she didn't think Mrs. Gooding would let her stay in the barn if she was rude to her. So she said nothing as she pushed back her anorak hood and shook her hair which was soaked with rain that dripped down her face.

The barn had a warm, sweet smell because of the hay stacked in bales against one of its walls. The chickens had come running in just before Dana and were spreading out in their never-ending search for this and that. One was crooning softly, between clucks, and the sound and the smell and the semi-gloom made the barn a place of welcome shelter, dispelling the anger that Dana had brought in with her.

'Oh, you've got rabbits!' she exclaimed, suddenly noticing the hutches behind Mrs. Gooding. 'Can I see them?'

'Help yourself. That black one, she's just had a litter. Fifteen of them.'

'Fifteen!'

'Well, fifteen that was. This little thing. . . .' She lifted her hand and showed a tiny black rabbit laid out on her palm. 'He won't last out the day. So it'll be fourteen.'

'What's the matter with him?'

'He's the runt. She won't have him. I've put him back three times but she keeps tossing him out.'

'What's a runt?'

'The one that's no good. There's nearly always one like that, weaker than all the rest, smaller, can't fend for himself.'

'Surely she'll look after that one more.'

Mrs. Gooding shook her head. 'Animals aren't like us. They don't want anything to do with runts or weaklings.'

'Is he still alive?' asked Dana. 'Can I hold him?' She rubbed her hands dry against her jersey.

His skin was like black velvet and he looked perfectly formed. But he was cold and even though she cupped him in both hands and willed her warmth into him, she could soon feel his coldness in her hands rather than transferring her warmth to him.

'Can I keep him? I'll look after him, really I will.'

'You can try, but it won't work. He's too young to be reared by hand.'

Dana didn't want to believe her. She sat down on one of the hay bales and tried and tried to bring warmth to the fragile life while waiting for the rain to stop. Mrs. Gooding was in a talkative mood and asked how they were getting on with their new life.

'What about that brother of yours? That's why you moved, isn't it, so he could have a better chance?'

Dana nodded, not wanting to talk about David. Couldn't she get away from him even on holiday? But Mrs. Gooding persisted.

'Well, is it doing him any good? Poor lad. It must be hard work for your mother, the care she takes of him.'

'How often will I have to feed him?' demanded Dana,

refusing to talk about David. 'What shall I give him?'

'Leave the poor little mite. Just keep him warm till he dies if it pleases you. That's the only comfort you can give him.'

'Why won't his mother look after him? I thought animals loved their babies, the same as humans.'

Mrs. Gooding shook her head. 'As soon as they're old enough to fend for themselves they forget about them. Birds throw their young ones out of the nest. Cats just walk off and leave their kittens. They have a natural instinct to protect their babies while they're helpless but they don't love them. Only humans know how to love.'

'Why?'

'Because people are made to be like God and animals aren't. He loves and he's made us able to love, too.'

'Do you believe in God?' asked Dana in surprise, remembering how she and Vicky had decided she was a witch.

'Of course I do. Don't you?'

'I don't know. How do you know God made us? How do you know he loves us?'

'Well, for one thing, it says so in the Bible. Don't you ever read the Bible?'

'I haven't got one.'

'That's a pity. Everyone should have a Bible. There wouldn't be so much trouble in the world if everyone read the Bible. Why do you suppose you care about that little rabbit? A minute ago you didn't even know he existed.'

Dana didn't have an answer to that question. She looked at him again. Was it because he was pretty. or helpless, or a baby? Why had her heart suddenly gone out to him, wanting to keep him alive even though Mrs. Gooding said he would die?

'I don't know,' she confessed.

'You see,' said Mrs. Gooding. 'If you read the Bible you'd know. God told us to look after the animals. He gave us a desire to care for them and protect them, and when you saw that little thing in need you wanted to help him.'

'But I can't. You've just said so.'

'True,' agreed Mrs. Gooding. 'Some things we have to leave in God's hands. He's the one who gives life and who takes it away again.'

'Can he change people?'

'He's the only one who can.'

Half in defiance, half scared, Dana said, 'I asked Jesus to change my brother but he hasn't done it.'

'Is that what you're angry about? I thought you were angry about something.'

'I'm angry about Jack, because he won't let me be friends with him,' insisted Dana, wishing Mrs. Gooding didn't know so much.

'I told you he wouldn't.'

'Yes, but I thought I could make him.'

'You were wrong.' After a pause she went on, 'Perhaps you're wrong about your brother, too, wanting him changed.'

'I thought Jesus could do miracles,' Dana defended herself, getting angry again. 'Isn't that what the Bible says?'

Mrs. Gooding replied more gently, 'Changing David would only be a little miracle. Changing you would be a much bigger one.'

That took Dana aback. 'Changing *me?*' she managed to ask, realising that Mrs. Gooding was repeating what Sandy's dad had already said, about wanting other people changed instead of wanting to be changed herself.

'Making you accept David as he is, loving him for who he is, how he is,' Mrs. Gooding explained. 'Of course Jesus can change him, but I dare say you're more in need than he is.'

In response to Dana's confused silence she went on, 'Aren't you a bit like that baby rabbit's mother, not wanting something that isn't the same as all the rest?'

The words hit Dana hard. She had never thought of it like that before, although there had been a time when David had just been David and she had loved him.

'Look at Jack,' went on Mrs. Gooding. 'He's a useless thing, eating his head off year in year out. But he doesn't bother me so I don't bother him. Why does everything have to be useful? Why can't animals, people, just be? Whose standard are we judging by, anyway?'

She sounded quite angry herself now and went on, 'But I can't stand here talking any longer. I've things to do.'

'Can I stay here a bit, till it stops raining?' asked Dana, not wanting to move.

'Stay as long as you like, but I must be off. Come to church tomorrow. It's Good Friday. Service at ten o'clock.'

With this she was gone, leaving Dana clutching the baby rabbit so still and cold in her palms.

She wondered if she might have a hanky to wrap him in, to keep him warmer, and started looking through her pockets, suddenly discovering the booklet Mr. Brent had given her and which she'd never read. There was no hanky and, anyway, it was too late. The baby rabbit was dead.

Carefully she laid him on a hay bale, feeling such a sense of sorrow for him though she didn't understand why until she remembered what Mrs. Gooding said about it being God who made people care about animals. Then it made sense. She realised that everything started to make sense when you related it to God.

Still thinking like this, she began looking at the booklet Mr. Brent had given her. It was a reminder of all the things he had told her about Jesus and there was a verse from the Bible.

'Some did receive him (Jesus) and believed in him, so he gave them the right to become God's children.'

God's children! What a good thought, to know you could belong to God like that, by saying yes to Jesus and going his way instead of her own.

It seemed as though Jesus was waiting for her to make up her mind right now, waiting for her answer in this quiet barn while the rain beat its steady reminder on the roof.

Was he really here? She knew he was. There was that same burning in her heart that she'd felt the night Mr. Brent had first talked to her about Jesus, and then again at the mission when she'd stood up to say yes to him before seeing her dad.

Suddenly she knew that Jesus had been wanting to come into her life for a long time, only she hadn't let him. She'd been too busy asking for things to be able to hear his voice, too much wanting things to go her way to be able to let him have his way.

'I'm sorry, Jesus,' she found herself whispering. 'I'm sorry for the way I feel about David, and all the mean things I've done, and for being angry with Fiona, and telling lies to Sandy and her mum and. . . .'

So many wrong things she'd said and done came into her mind one after the other while she sat on the hay bale and she kept saying 'sorry' until after a while the memories stopped and a great weight seemed lifted from her heart.

'Jesus, will you please change me? Make me love you and David and Mum and Dad, the way you want me to love them. And Fiona and Sandy and. . . .'

It seemed there were a lot of people she'd been mean to and she knew when she'd finished thinking of everybody, even Mrs. Hayward and Mrs. Lewis, that Jesus had somehow put her right with them all.

To her surprise, too, she realised that she'd been praying in a way she'd never have thought of for herself and that Jesus had given her all the words to say; that somehow he was there, loving her, and everything was all right. She didn't know whether she wanted to laugh or cry, but she knew for certain that she'd got herself right with him.

That night, during the midnight feast which consisted of several chocolate bars, a tin of peaches, a packet of cream biscuits, two bags of crisps and a bottle of orange, Dana told Vicky about Jesus.

Vicky had borrowed an alarm clock so they could wake up at exactly midnight and they talked and even giggled in whispers so as not to disturb Vicky's parents. Opening the peach tin was hard work. Neither of them were used to tin openers. Then they realised they'd forgotten plates and spoons so they took it in turns to eat slices of dripping peach with their fingers which somehow made it taste much nicer than usual. Peach juice slid up their arms and down their chins, but that too was fun, and for a long time they talked about different kinds of food, both gorgeous and revolting, until they could eat no more and began to feel a bit sick.

They crept to the bathroom to wash off all the stickiness and Vicky thought cleaning their teeth again would be a good idea (she had been to the dentist that morning!). Then she said they could tell each other ghost stories till they fell asleep.

She'd been given permission to light a candle, which made strange shadows on the walls, and they jumped back into bed because it was cold. For a while they just watched the candle, such a bright light in the darkness all around. The idea of the candle was to make things creepy, but its steady flame gave Dana a feeling of warmth and comfort. She wanted to tell Vicky about Jesus but she didn't know how to start and she found herself silently praying, 'Please, Jesus, show me how to tell Vicky.'

Vicky had gone quiet, too. Was she feeling sick? She'd been groaning earlier on and saying she'd never eat any more chocolate, ever. Perhaps she'd fallen asleep. Dana was beginning to feel sleepy herself.

Suddenly Vicky said, 'That candle reminds me of a song we used to sing at Sunday School when I was little, before you used to come.'

She began singing softly, 'Jesus bids us shine with a pure clear light, like a little candle shining in the night. . . . Um. . . . Can't remember the rest.'

'Do you believe in Jesus?' Dana asked and, hardly waiting for Vicky's reply, she rushed into telling her about Sandy and Mr. Brent and saying the wrong kind of prayers until Jesus showed her how to say the right kind. It was all a muddle, she was in such a hurry to tell it all, and when she'd finished Vicky was silent for such a long time that she thought she'd fallen asleep and hadn't heard anything.

'Vicky. . . . ?'

'Um?'

'Did you hear what I said?'

'Mm.'

'Well?'

'Oh, let's blow the candle out and go to sleep. I'm tired,' and Vicky jumped out of bed, puffed hard against the flame and plunged them into darkness. 'Night,' she said and that was that.

The next day was Good Friday, the day Jesus had died, and Dana remembered what Mrs. Gooding had said about going to church. Vicky's family was going. Nearly everybody in the village went to church for Easter, Harvest and Christmas.

Dana's heart thumped with excitement as she went up the familiar church path, remembering how she liked to go there on her own to look at the windows and enjoy the stillness. She remembered, too, how she and Vicky used to giggle their way through the Sunday School lessons and how Vicky hadn't said anything in response to her confession in the middle of the night.

To her surprise Dana didn't find the service boring at

all. She really wanted to understand what was going on and so she listened attentively to the Bible readings instead of letting her mind wander and heard the story of how Jesus was taken before Pilate and Herod and how all the crowd who had loved him before cried, 'Away with him. Crucify him.'

She listened, too, to what the vicar had to say about why such a terrible Friday should be called 'good' and for the first time understood how she herself had been involved in that crucifixion such a long, long time ago. There was such a mixture of joy, sorrow and wonder in her heart as she heard it all and joined in the Easter hymns that afterwards Vicky said to her somewhat rudely, 'You looked really silly, crying in church.'

She couldn't help feeling glad that she was going home the next day. Things with Vicky weren't the same any more and she knew it was because she had told her about Jesus. However, rather than feeling angry with Vicky, she found herself thinking, 'I must ask Jesus to change Vicky, too, like he's changed me.'

Mrs. Gooding had waved to her and, on the way out of church, said, 'You're not looking angry any more,' and Dana knew that she wasn't because Jesus had taken all her anger away.

10

Dana had bought herself some comics to read on the long journey home but once she'd finished them she found herself thinking about David, wondering why she had been so ashamed of him that she'd wanted to pretend he didn't exist.

She started remembering all the nice things about him, the way his face always lit up when he first saw her each morning or when he came home from the Centre; the way he wanted to share everything with her and was quite happy to push his newest toys on her the minute she exclaimed how nice they were; the way he always wanted to please her.

From what the girls at school said, she knew that David was a much nicer person than some of their brothers. And the more she thought about him, the more she longed to see him again and try to make up to him for having ignored him for so long.

She was keen to see Sandy again, too, to share with her all that had happened. Tomorrow was Sunday. Would Mum let her go to church with Sandy? She was going to ask her anyway. And she was going to get out that poster and stick it up on her wall and invite Sandy to tea, and Fiona, too, if she'd come. . . .

Mum, Dad and David were all waiting for her at the bus station and there were hugs and kisses as if she'd been away for a year instead of just a week. It seemed like a year to Dana. She was so glad to be back and she let David hold her hand all the way home in the car while she told him about Jack and Fred and the baby rabbit and answered all Mum and Dad's questions, too.

'You never told us about that pony!' exclaimed Mum.

'It was a secret,' explained Dana. 'But it doesn't matter. I would never have tamed him. He's not that sort of pony. Jack's got a mind of his own.'

'Like Mrs. Gooding,' laughed Dad.

'And Fred,' said Mum. 'What an awful creature that goose is. I remember when I went there for some eggs one day. . . .', and she told how she had been chased by Fred right out of Mrs. Gooding's yard.

'Any more secrets?' asked Dad jokingly when she'd finished and almost shyly Dana replied, 'Yes, but I'll tell you when we get home. It's a really important one.'

'Mm. That sounds serious,' said Mum.

'Dana come home,' said David, grinning at her and stroking her arm.

'We've all missed you but David's missed you most of all,' said Dad. 'He's done nothing but talk about you all day and he's drawn a picture for you.'

'Drawn a picture,' repeated David. 'Picture for Dana.'

As soon as they were inside the front door he started dragging her into the living room where his picture was. It was a really big one, done with poster paints on brown paper, and it didn't take Dana more than a few moments to realise that it was a picture of Noah's ark with some animals that might have been lions or sheep or perhaps donkeys, or all three, waiting to go inside. Noah, with a long beard, was pointing the way and over all a rainbow with three stripes glowed down.

'He did it ever so carefully,' began Mum protectively in the face of Dana's silence.

'It's lovely,' said Dana. 'I couldn't have had a better coming home present.' Everyone could see she meant it and David waggled his head with joy. 'Can I put it on my wall? David can help me. Come on, David. Let's do it right now.'

She helped pull him up the stairs, found some blue tack, and showed David how to roll it up in his fingers to make it soft so that it would stick to the paper. When they'd put up his picture she pulled Sandy's poster from under the wardrobe and stuck it up next to it.

'Nice,' said David. 'Sheep.'

'Do you want to know what it says?' Dana asked, and when he nodded she told him. She told him, too, that the person you had to seek was Jesus and that when you looked for him you found him because he was really there.

'I've found him,' she said. 'And I'm going to tell you all about him so you can find him, too.'

Dad was in the doorway. He must have heard her.

'Mum's got the kettle on,' he said. 'Are you two coming down for tea?'

'Nice picture,' said David, wanting Dad to look at Sandy's poster.

'Dad, I was at that meeting. The one you were at. I saw you.' The words burst out of Dana. She didn't want there to be any more secrets.

'I know. Mr. Brent told me. A lot of things have happened while you've been away.'

'They've happened to me, too.'

She flung herself into his arms and they stood hugging each other, not needing to say anything. Then David put his arms round them both, wanting to be part of it, and they all laughed as they held on to each other and David was the only one who wasn't surprised. He enjoyed expressing his feelings.

'Does Mum know?' Dana asked.

Dad nodded.

'Does she mind?'

He shrugged. 'You know Mum. Sandy's parents came round one evening. We had a long talk. They're nice people. She likes them, but it's going to take time. Don't try to rush her. She still thinks it's a lot of nonsense.'

'It isn't though, is it, Dad?'

'No,' he agreed. 'It's real, though I can still hardly believe it. I'm a changed person.'

'I think I am too,' said Dana.

'Are you coming down for tea?' Mum shouted up the stairs. 'There's a chocolate cake just asking to be eaten.'

'Chocolate!' exclaimed David, his face lighting up, and soon they were all round the table enjoying the tea which Mum had obviously prepared specially for Dana's homecoming, with her favourite tuna fish sandwiches, lettuce and tomato and trifle, as well as the chocolate cake.

'So what's your secret?' asked Mum when they'd done justice to all the food and David had quietened down and got used to having Dana home again.

Dana found herself going very red. 'It's Jesus,' she said.

Mum didn't sound terribly surprised. 'That's what comes of mixing with religious people,' she said in an 'I told you so' voice. 'You and Sandy. Dad and that man at the garage. The Brents. They brainwash you. You believe anything they tell you.'

'But it's true, Mum. Even if I never saw Sandy again or never went to church again or anything, it'd still be true. Jesus would still be real.'

'You sound just like Dad!'

Dana didn't know if she was cross or not. She and Dad must have done a lot of talking while she was away if she could take it so calmly.

'You won't stop me going to church with Sandy, will you? I want so much to go,' she rushed on. 'I went yesterday and it was lovely. But I won't go if you don't want me to.'

'What, and have you miserable all day! You'd better go but don't expect me to come along.'

The next day David wanted to go to church, too. He clung to Dana as though she were going to disappear again and the only way to calm him was by letting him

90

go, too.

It was Easter Sunday and the church was packed with people who had come to share the joy of knowing that Jesus had risen from the dead and was alive for evermore. The hymns and choruses, all so new to Dana, gave her the words she needed to express what she felt and yet didn't know how to say, and it was good to sing out at the top of her voice with everyone else, 'He's alive, he's alive, he's alive.'

David liked this chorus, too, and he joined in, a bit behind everyone else. Instead of spoiling, it somehow added to the general sense of joy. Dana glanced at him, holding his song book upside down, standing a bit lopsided between her and Dad but thoroughly enjoying himself.

With a stab of surprise in her heart she saw a different David. Not the little brother she protected and amused and loved; not the clumsy, embarrassing half-adult who didn't fit in and cramped her life, but a person who had thoughts and feelings of his own, someone Jesus loved and who could love Jesus.

It was almost as big a discovery as finding Jesus and she was thrown into confusion. She'd never seen David like this before, just being himself, doing what he wanted to do rather than what people tried to get him to do because it was good for him. She couldn't explain what was different about him. Perhaps he wasn't different at all, but that she was seeing him with new eyes.

David went home with a big grin on his face, still trying to sing the choruses and very much determined to tell Mum all about it. Dana and Mr. Hughes didn't need to say anything at all.

Going back to school after Easter wasn't easy. There was that mingled anticipation and dread which started every new term but on top of that was not knowing how to react to Fiona when she saw her again. She'd talked to Sandy about Fiona and talked to Jesus about her, too.

She wanted so much to make friends with her again, but in a different way.

She wasn't going to pretend about ponies any more. She wanted to be honest and straight with her but, underneath the wanting, was the memory that Fiona could be very cruel, and there was still the smart of humiliation she had felt when Fiona told everyone about David.

Dana didn't know how these things could be put right but she remembered Sandy's favourite verse, 'Don't be afraid' and another one that said, 'I'll be with you always'. So, although she prepared to face Fiona with a sinking feeling in her stomach, there was also the certainty in her heart that somehow Jesus would sort it all out.

Fiona wasn't in the classroom and she didn't come to school all that week. On the Friday Dana asked the teacher what had happened to her and heard that she'd gone off to America with her father and that it wasn't certain if she'd be coming back. Everyone was surprised because Fiona hadn't mentioned it to anyone or even said goodbye to her friends.

Dana still had Fiona's address so on the Saturday she and Sandy went to see if they could find out anything about her, especially her new address so that Dana could write.

Fiona's home turned out to be a bedsit that she shared with her mother in a converted Victorian house shared by at least eight other people. Only the landlady was in. She told them off for pressing all the bells but afterwards was quite willing to inform them that Fiona had indeed gone off with her father and that the first her mother knew about it was when a cable came from America telling her it had happened.

'Serve her right, too, the stuck-up thing,' added the landlady with satisfaction. 'All her airs and graces and half the time she can't pay the rent.'

Dana and Sandy were glad to get away from her. Dana's heart ached for Fiona who had told as many lies as she had and whose family was so broken up. It was good to be able to share what they had learned with Mrs. Brent, to sit round the kitchen table together and pray for Fiona and her parents and know that Jesus cared for them whether they knew anything about him or not.

'Perhaps I'll go and talk to Fiona's mum,' said Mrs. Brent when they'd finished praying. 'I expect she needs someone to share things with.'

Dana was comforted. Mrs. Brent wouldn't mind about her being stuck up. She was good at talking to people.

'I wish you'd talk to my mum, too,' she blurted out.

'All in good time,' she said. 'The Bible tells us that there's a time for everything, and the worst thing is to try to rush things.'

Sandy grinned. 'Remember when my dad put out those lettuces? You know, when you first talked to him? Well, they all died. He put them out too soon.'

'Only because he was in a hurry. Another couple of weeks would have made all the difference,' agreed Mrs. Brent.

'It was Chocolate's fault really,' admitted Sandy. 'He kept knocking the pot off the windowsill and Dad was fed up with him, so he put them in the garden.'

'Is it too soon for my mum then?' asked Dana, wishing it wasn't because she longed so much to be able to share Jesus with her.

'Not to worry,' comforted Mrs. Brent. 'A lot of things have happened already, haven't they, and the wonderful thing about Jesus is that he never stops doing wonderful things. You just be patient and go on praying. It'll all happen when the time is right. People are more important than lettuces.'

Dana and Sandy laughed. They were both learning that, even with Jesus, there weren't always easy answers to things. Things didn't happen just because you wanted them to, or when you wanted them to. Knowing that he cared was the main thing. Knowing that he could do the impossible just made it more exciting.

The weeks went by but Mum continued tight and offputting whenever Dana tried to talk to her about Jesus. She wouldn't listen to Dad, either, as far as Dana could see. However, there was David. Mum couldn't ignore David and David couldn't understand why Mum who shared everything with him didn't want to share all his new friends and the songs he sang.

A curious battle was going on between them with David constantly trying to drag Mum to church on Sunday mornings and having to be prevented by Dad, and Mum trying to persuade David to stay at home with her. Neither would give way.

'Why is Mum so stubborn?' Dana cried impatiently to Dad one day. 'Why won't she just come once to please David? She's always wanting to please him in everything else.'

Dad laughed.

'What's so funny?'

'Not so long ago you were moaning because everything was to please David,' he remarked. 'Now you're cross because he's not getting what he wants!'

It was true. And Dana had to laugh too.

In the end, of course, David got his way. Very reluctantly, and only as a special favour to David, did Mum agree to go to church one day, 'Just this once,' she insisted. David was able to show the delight that Dana and Mr. Hughes felt but kept to themselves as, instead of waving them goodbye, she got into the car with them.

She didn't sing a single hymn or say a single prayer but she did start talking to people afterwards and Dana actually saw her smiling.

On the way home Dana heard Dad say to Mum, 'It wasn't so bad, was it?' and Mum somewhat stiffly agreed, 'I suppose not.'

Dana grinned at David and squeezed his hand. He could do things that she couldn't.

'Oh, thank you, Jesus,' she said in her heart.